The Seeds of LIFE

by
TYRONE FITZGERALD,
MICHAEL L, LEWIS SR.,
ANDRE CARR
Platinum Plus Inc.

ISBN 978-1-962363-84-6 (Paperback)
ISBN 978-1-962363-85-3 (Ebook)

Inquiries and Book Orders should be addressed to:

Leavitt Peak Press
17901 Pioneer Blvd Ste L #298, Artesia, California 90701
Phone #: 2092191548

CHAPTER ONE

"THE SEED OF LIFE"

ALABAMA- 1956

INT: THE DEPUTIES ARE DRIVING ON A DUSTY DIRT MILE LONG DRIVEWAY THAT RUNS ALONG THE TENNESSEE RIVER THREW THICK SMOKE FROM TREES AND NEARBY BUSHES SET ON FIRE.

THE DEPUTIES DRIVING UP THEIR DUSTY DRIVEWAY 1 MILE LONG ROAD APPROACHING, AT NORMAL SPEED, THROUGH THE THICK SMOKE FROM TREES NEAR THE RIVER. FRIGHTENED NEIGHBORS WATCH WHILE THE FOLLOWING TOOK PLACE:

FREDERICK WHO WAS BRUTALLY TORMENTED AND FRIGHTENED, FINALLY SEES THE DEPUTIES AND GOES TO LET THEM KNOW HOW THE NIGHT STARTED – AT WHAT GURESOME HORROR HIS FAMILY ENTAILED…:

EARLY EVENING- COOL QUIET TOWN OF ALABAMA, 1956
Fred and his wife, Sadie, share the house with his parents. In the living room, Sadie, who is pregnant with her and Fred's first child, practice scales on their piano. Fred closes his eyes. He visualizes the posters again, the ones plastered throughout the county by the KU

KLUX KLAN who's seeking to maintain many features or prewar restrictions. "KILL ALL THE FREED SLAVES!" "KILL THE NIGGERS!" Each accusing word, Frederick Harris believes, is directed at his family.

SURELY EVERYONE IN THE COUNTRY KNEW THAT FREDERICK HARRIS' GRANDFATHER WAS A FIELD SLAVE BEFORE THE RATIFICATION OF THE 13TH AMENDMENT IN 1865. THE COUNTY NEIGHBORS WERE ALSO AWARE THAT FRED'S GRANDMOTHER WAS DOCTOR, BORN A FREE SLAVE IN NORTH CAROLINA IN 1900. FRED'S FATHER IS A MINISTER, AND WORST OF ALL, HE PROTESTED AGAINST THE BRUTAL BEHAVIOR OF THE KU KLUX KLAN.

THAT EVENING, AS FRED'S FATHER PREPARED TO GO OUT TO TAKE CARE OF SOME BUSINESS DOWN AT THE CHURCH, HE WALKS OUT ONTO THE PORCH TO SAY GOODNIGHT TO FRED.

Okay, Frederick, I should be back in a couple of hours I hope but, you know where I keep my guns, I don't you.

But poop, ah, it's getting dark, do
you think it's a good idea to be
going out this evening? Aren't you
afraid the Klan will come out
tonight?

Ah, er, son, er, I really don't
know. I don't think anyone knows
when they'll come. Don't worry,
ah, er, don't worry about it.

FRED

But pop, ah, you know they're
getting close. The Ku Klux Klan
just burned another house down and
hung the owners from their front
yard tree together.

MINISTER

Uh, uh, er, Fred, sure, there's
always that possibility they'll
come but, I don't believe so. I'm
not afraid son, no, I don't think
they will.

FRED

Well, pop, if you don't think the
Klan will come, let's throw all
Those guns of yours in the river.
You know mother is so afraid of
those guns in the house, pop, she
keeps trying to get me to get rid
of them.

MINISTER
(he rushes off and hops in
his car and speeds away.)

Moments pass, a strange and muffled noise drowns out the river's
drainage. Fred starts reading his school books. The music from inside
the house stops. Fred quickly closes his book and freeze in his position, and listens to menacing shouts, growing louder and louder.

He drops his book, jumps up quickly, and runs through the house
to the back-kitchen window facing the woos. Suddenly, the dark

wooded area starts to fill with a couple of glowing fire crosses. A surging small crowd of angry men wearing black hooded robes appear and shouting.

KLANSMEN

SHOUTING

"KILL THE NIGGERS, KILL THE
NIGGERS, KILL THE NIGGERS!"

As the surging klansmen start to walk faster towards the house, Fred suddenly hears other menacing shouts coming from within the house. Fred spins quickly around and runs back into the living room to see a Klansman ordering three others to search the house. As Fred stands watching them, a Klansman sneaks up behind him and sticks a gun to the side of Fred's head.

KLANSMAN

Move another inch Nigger.

KLANSMAN

and I'll blow your nappy-ass head off!
Fred freezes in his tracks,
hands in the air, his eyes
stretched with fear, and with
practiced precision, the
Klansmen worked their way from
the first floor to the attic,
looking for any item of luxury.
The Klansmen overturn all
the wooden dressers, they took
everything personal, valuable
out of the house.

KLANSMEN

That's right, Nigger, now you'll
understand, you can't enjoy this
kind of life. People like y'all
are not supposed to live like this!

Moments pass, stunned, the
family begins to straighten the
mess. But suddenly, a second
wave of Klansmen, this time
they are wearing white hooded
robes and masks, and gloves
too, storm the house. Though it
looks as if there is nothing
more to take, they rush out of
the house carrying Fred, and
his father's suits, coats and
pants. As they are leaving,
two of the Klansmen see Sadie
sitting at the piano, scared
stiff, they approach her.

FRED
(Suddenly screams at the Klansman.)
No, please sir, don't hurt my wife!
Please, what more do you want?

(He is subdued when a
knife is poked gently in
his back.)

KLANSMAN

Freeze Nigger, or I'll cut your heart
out, mother-fucker!

FRED

But, sir, please, don't hurt
my wife, what more do you want?
My wife is having a baby.
Our first baby, please, sir. Don't
let them hurt her!

KKK- FURIOUSLY – LAUGHING PUSH SADIE TO FLOOR TO GET PIANO.

THE KLANSMEN IGNORES FRED'S CRY AND PUSHES SADIE OFF OF THE PIANO BENCH ONTO THE FLOOR AS THEY ROLL THE SMALL PIANO OUT OF THE HOUSE, PUSHES IT DOWN THE STEPS, AND LAUGHS. THEY RUN BACK INSIDE TO RETRIEVE THE MAHOGANY CHAIRS AND DRESSERS THAT THE FIRST GROUP OF KLANSMAN AHD KNOCKED OVER ON THE FLOOR. THE HARRIS FAMILY IS HELPLESS. THEY HUDDLE IN THE CORNER OF THE ROOM AND STARE IN DISBELIEF. NO ONE CRIES, NO ONE SPEAKS, NO ONE MOVES.

MOMENTS PAST, SILENTLY, SLOWLY, THE FAMILY MEMBERS PICK THROUGH THE RUBBLE THAT IS THEIR HOME, TRYING TO RESTORE ORDER TO WORLD THAT IS ONLY BEGINNING TO COLLAPSE.

Suddenly, a rock crashes through the living room window as a third group of white male teenagers start vandalizing the house from the outside itself. One of the teenagers' spray paint nasty slurs on the walls. Another had already started a fire out in front of the house and begun to toss broken piano pieces into the fire.

Finally, they appear- the Deputies at 10p.m. from the Sheriff's Department to investigate the Harris family complaint. Some of the neighborhood parents and children watch in fear outside of their houses behind some tall hedges along the road.

DEPUTY SMITH

Slowly walks around the living room at the damages with a pen and report log in hands, smiling as he speaks.)

> Ah, we received your call, and
> sorry we're late, but, ah, ah, can
> anyone explains to Deputy Jones and
> me what happened? We need to make
> a report.

FRED

> Are you serious sir! Look at this
> fucking place! It sure wasn't a
> damn earthquake.

DEPUTY SMITH

> But, first, sir, I need your name
> For my report.

FRED

> Frederick Harris, sir, Frederick
> Harris

DEPUTY SMITH

> Okay, sir, could you explain to me
> and Deputy Jones what happen sir?
> What I mean, can you describe to us
> how the persons look who done this?

He walks around the room again looking
at the damage, smiles at Deputy Jones

FRED
(Snaps angrily)

What, who done this? Are you
really serious, deputy, the fucking
Ku Klux Klan, that's who! This
kind of shit happens all the time
around here, and you know that too.
I shouldn't have to explain
anything to you!

DEPUTY SMITH

Hey Jones, you believe that, the
Klan?

FRED

Fucking right, sir, the Klan!
They're running around the fucking
South, looting, robbing, raping,
and killing our people like it's a
fucking sport! And not a damn
thing is being done about it
either!

DEPUTY JONES

Ah, Mr. Harris, and you saying
these hooded suspects were wearing
gloves too.

Of course, gentlemen, they

destroyed everything! They even
rolled my wife's piano out of my
parent's house down the fucking
front steps!

DEPUTY JONES

Your parent's house, Mr. Harris?
Um, ah, I thought you lived here?

FRED

Yes, I do, ah, we do. My wife over
there sitting in the corner of the
room, we're both living here until
I get my call to start my new job
with the railroad. Then we're
moving up near the white folks, if
you're that concerned sir.

DEPUTY JONES
(Stares at Deputy Smith, he stares back)

Well, sir, you really think and
your wife should be moving over
there? I don't think you people
are wanted over on that side of the
county. A lot of strange things
happen over there near the new
highway extension. From what I
understand, Mr. Harris, they're
planning to move all the coloreds
living near.

DEPUTY SMITH

That's all right Mr. Harris, this
is a free country. You and your
wife have the right to live
anywhere you like! But, sir, why
is your wife sitting on the floor?

FREDERICK HARRIS

Oh, Sadie, the baby, are you okay?

SADIE HARRIS

That's okay Freddy, I think I'm
alright. The baby and I are fine.

DEPUTY SMITH

But, Mr. Harris, you really expect
me and Deputy Jones to put this in
our report that the Ku Klux Klan
did this, and you're still alive to
talk about it
Yeah, and Smith, I guess it's too
code for a hanging.

CHAPTER TWO

IT WAS SATURDAY, JUNE 20, 1956, THE DAY AFTER THE SCHOOL TERM HAD ENDED THAT JEFFREY O'NEAL, A LEXINGTON ALABAMA HIGH SCHOOL HISTORY TEACHER, HAD STARTED HIS SUMMER JOB AT THE DINER, WHEN HE GOT THE CALL FROM BETTY. AS SOON AS SHE SAID HER NAME AND JEFFREY HEARD THE DESPERATION IN HER VOICE, HE KNEW EXACTLY WHAT HAD HAPPENED.

Oh, Jeffrey, oh God, Jeffrey, they
found her nude body hanging from a
tree in back of the school yard.
And, er, er, Jeffrey, I don't know
what to do? I received a phone
call from the Sheriff's Department
and the deputies are on their way
here looking for Patrick Sullivan.

Jeffrey O'Neal sits on the counter
stool with the phone
pressed up against his shoulder
and ear, slowly rotating side
to side, stares at himself in the
mirror thinking to himself.
He slowly closes his eyes as he
continues to rotate thinking
to himself until Betty shouts
in a loud voice snapping

Jeffrey out of his thoughts.

Jeffrey, are you there? Did you
hear what I said, Deborah Harris
from Running Creek County is dead
Jeffrey-

(Suddenly awakes from his thoughts)
Ah, yeah, Betty, ah, I heard you,
but, ah, ah, my mind have just been
blown to shits. I just hope it's

JEFFREY O'NEAL (cont'd)
not true. I hope he really didn't
stoop that low.

Stoop that low, Jeffrey, what the
hell are you talking about? Who in
the hell are you talking about
Jeffrey?

Jeffrey O'Neal, knew Deborah
Harris's death was not an ordinary
hanging by the Ku Klux Klan. Jeffrey
had been listening to Patrick
Sullivan predicting Deborah's death
for the last nine months, but
hadn't believed it. Jeffrey O'Neal
was absolutely certain he knew
too, who the MURDERER WAS!

During the school term, one day
at lunch, Patrick had even
told Jeffrey how this person was
going to hang Deborah

Harris, which tree, and on what
day, but, the prediction was
so bizarre, so ludicrous, that
Jeffrey hadn't taken it
seriously. Now, as the reality
tore through his guts, he
felt numb.

Jeffrey O'Neal had been raised
an Anglo Catholic. His
mother, would punish Jeffrey if
he was caught playing with
the Negro children. Jeffrey was
not a shy child, he spoke
against slavery at a very young
age. But punishment affected
Jeffrey emotionally. So, he learned
to use his playtime with
his make-believe friends to
relieve any anxiety.

Jeffrey enjoyed jumping off of
his special rock into the
river. He though of that rock
as the center of his world.
it made, he learned to
reasoned, four quadrants:

1. In the first quadrant, he'd grow up and protest
   against slavery;

2. In the second, he'd get married to a Negro girl
   and make lots and lots of Negro babies;

3. He'd become President and lock up the Ku Klux
   Klan forever, perhaps, whip them and hang them

in trees so everyone could see, so they'll know what it's like to hang his Negro friend's parents,

4. He would move away with his Negro friends back to Africa, near a swimming hole, so they could swim all day long without anyone interfering. When Jeffrey jumped off his rock into the river as a child, he always promised himself that he'll always be the best white friend a Negro could have.

IMPORTANT: NIGHT- CAR- RIGHT AFTER WORK

Music in the car softly playing- Fate Domino

JEFFREY IS IN A DAZE AND CAN THINK ONLY OF DEBRA'S LYNCHING-HE MUST SPEAK TO PATRICK DRIVING IN THE SUMMER HEAT.

Jeffrey feels a desperate need to talk to Patrick Sullivan, and tell him that he had been right all along about Deborah's lynching, but, couldn't believe, John Johnson, the principal of the school where he, Patrick Sullivan, Betty, and Deborah Harris had taught classes, had actually committed the murder. Jeffrey also felt that he had better warn Patrick to be careful and watch out for the Ku Klux Klan. Jeffrey retold the conversation he had with Patrick the last time he spoke to him at school about the principal's plot to kill Deborah Harris.

JEFFREY O'NEAL

But, Patrick, if you really think
the Principal is going to commit a
murder to one of his own teaching
staff members, why not involve the
sheriff?

PATRICK SULLIVAN

Can you imagine that, Jeffrey, me,
a white teacher going to the
sheriff's office to snitch on my
boss? Be realistic Jeffrey,
Deborah's a Negro woman from
Running Creek County, Alabama,
somewhere, what good would it do?
If anything, I'll be the one who
would get my ass chewed out.

JEFFREY O'NEAL

So what, Patrick, Deborah was a
friend

PATRICK SULLIVAN

So what? Jeffrey, be realistic,
John Johnson has all sorts of
contacts down here in Lexington,
Alabama. They'll investigate,

PATRICK SULLIVAN (cont'd)
Consider Deborah's death another
statistic, and then, Jeffrey,
they'll find out who ratted on the
principal, and, ah, ah, then I'll
probably be found floating face
down in the fucking river!

But, so what if John Johnson has
these so called contacts, Patrick,
that's not the point! Ah, whether
we're in danger or not, and, I'll

tell you what difference it does
make. IT'S MURDER! If we don't
stand up for equal rights for the
Negroes then, Patrick, we'll die as
a nation!

(Sighs)
Look Jeffrey, I understand how you
feel about your Negro buddies but,
I personally, do not need any
confrontation. I have to live and
work here-

JEFFREY O'NEAL

INTERRUPTS ANGRILY

What, Patrick, you don't want to
get involve? But, you know
yourself, Patrick, that Deborah was
a hell of a school teacher! She
was the most thoughtful, sweetest
person in the world. She wouldn't
hurt a fly.

PATRICK SULLIVAN
(Sighs)

LOOK, JEFFREY, I UNDERSTAND THAT TOO, BUT HOW
WILL THAT LOOK? THINK ABOUT OUR REPUTATIONS,
OUR JOBS. IF THEY FOUND OUT THAT JOHN JOHNSON,
MURDERED ONE OF HIS OWN MEMBERS OF HIS
TEACHING STAFF, THE CREDIBILITY OF ONE OF THE
BEST SCHOOLS IN LEXINGTON, ALABAMA, WOULD BE
SHOT!

JEFFREY O'NEAL
Are you talking about credibility,
Patrick? Who the fuck you think we
should give all the credibility to
for all the dead Negroes the
sheriffs and deputies find
scattered around Alabama like
trash.

PATRICK SULLIVAN

Well, ah, ah, the Ku Klux Klan, I
guess, Jeffrey, but, we have to be
very careful we don't step on the
wrong person's shoes. Think about
our reputations if this gets out ot
the press, Jeffrey!

JEFFREY O'NEAL

PAUSES, EYES AND MOUTH WIDE OPEN.

I can't believe you Patrick. A
human being's life has just been
snatched from beneath her eyes
because of someone's ignorance, and
you're more concern with the
credibility of the school's
reputation!

PATRICK SULLIVAN

What, my own blind prejudice? I'm
not prejudice, Jeffrey, how could
you say that? I'm quite sure you
know I've even gotten a piece of

ass from Deborah when she was alive! (Giggles.) As a matter of fact, a few times.

JEFFREY O'NEAL

(Interrupts)

But that has nothing to do with it, Patrick!

PATRICK SULLIVAN

(Snickers)

Oh yeah, why not? If you claim this blind prejudice bull shit is true, and you know how I think, sir, then why would I have screwed her if I'm so prejudice?

JEFFREY O'NEAL

But, sex has nothing to do with your own guilt Patrick! Just because you have sex with a person doesn't mean you necessarily like that person, or not prejudice.

(Pause, giggle's.)

I guess you do have a point to a certain extent, Patrick.

PATRICK SULLIVAN

(Interrupts)

I do?

JEFFREY O'NEAL

Yes, you do, because unloved sex is
just a motion. It doesn't
discriminate.

PATRICK SULLIVAN
(Sighs, slowly shakes head side to side.)

You know, Jeffrey, you are starting
to really worry me. But, look,
Jeffrey, I felt sorry for Deborah,
and all the hatred she was getting
from the principal, but she
wouldn't listen. She kept on
insisting to teach her history
class her way, and not the right
way John Johnson wanted her out. To
Leave.

JEFFREY O'NEAL

But, the right way, Patrick, what
the hell are you talking about?

PATRICK SULLIVAN

Come on Jeffrey, you're an English
teacher, read the writing between
the lines.

JEFFREY O'NEAL
But, I still don't know where you
are coming from, Patrick.

PATRICK SULLIVAN
(Interrupts)

Come on, Jeffrey, you know how
Deborah Harris taught her history
class. She didn't follow John
Johnson's rules. She taught Negro
history to white students! Now
isn't that obscene, Jeffrey?

JEFFREY O'NEAL

Obscene? Not, really Patrick.
What's so obscene about teaching,
and showing how the Negroes were,
and still are treated today in
white America, to her white
students?

PATRICK SULLIVAN
(Snickers)

Well, Jeffrey, I don't know about this
day and age, 1956, but maybe in
the year 2001 or 2005, maybe things
will change by then, but Deborah
kept including in her lesson plans
that the white students should
realize that all slaves weren't dumb
and ignorant. She even told the
principal, Jeffrey, himself. That she
didn't give a damn, her students
will be taught the achievements and
contributions the Negroes gave to
the building of America.

JEFFREY O'NEAL

Well, I'll be the master's slave,
Patrick. But isn't it true,
shouldn't the white students learn
more about the Negroes, other than
being told that they're nothing
more but, for sale, to be slaved,
and raped, and slaughtered?

PATRICK SULLIVAN

Come on Jeffrey, you know what I
mean, don't you?

JEFFREY O'NEAL
(Smiles)

Not really, Patrick, tell me then?

PATRICK SULLIVAN
(Sighs)

Well, alright, you see, Jeffrey,
Deborah just taught American
history her way. She said the
history books lied, and it only
showed the white kids that slavery
was the proper way to treat the
Negroes

JEFFREY O'NEAL
(Interrupts)

Wait, ah, I guess you have a point
there, Patrick. I guess Deborah

couldn't have taught history any other way but, the John Johnson way?

PATRICK SULLIVAN
(Smiles)

Now do you see where I'm coming from Jeffrey? All Deborah use to teach was about the freed slaves, you know, about their rights, religion, and that all Negroes should have the same rights as white people. Now, if Deborah was so concerned about human rights, she should have elaborated on the white mens accomplishments to America.

JEFFREY O'NEAL

Ah, Patrick, wasn't Deborah talking about the Emancipation Proclamation? Wasn't she was a firm believer in the 13th Amendment, and the establishment of the Freeman's Bureau, in 1865 in Washington DC?

PATRICK SULLIVAN

Yes she was, Jeffrey, but that's not right, and John Johnson was furious because he told Deborah over and over that her lesson plans should not include the 13th Amendment.

JEFFREY O'NEAL
(Confused)

Ah, it shouldn't? But that's
ridiculous, Patrick, it's in the
history books. It has been
documented too! I don't understand
why the principal doesn't want it
discussed to the students?

PATRICK SULLIVAN

That's simple, Jeffrey, read
between the lines, because the 13th
amendment applied to the entire
country!

JEFFREY O'NEAL
(Hunched shoulders, smiles)

So, what's wrong with that?

PATRICK SULLIVAN

I'll tell you what's wrong with
that, Jeffrey, that Emancipation
Proclamation applied then, only to
areas outside of Union control!

JEFFREY O'NEAL
(Smiling)

Oh yeah, that's right. But weren't
the Black Codes kind of different
in each state?

PATRICK SULLIVAN

I ah, guess so.

JEFFREY O'NEAL

You don't sound to sure of
yourself. Why not?

PATRICK SULLIVAN

Well, the Negroes couldn't vote,
they couldn't hold any office, or
serve on any jury of testify
against any white man. They still
can't assemble without official
permission. But, ah, Jeffrey, you
are really starting to worry me.
Why in the hell are you bringing up
"shit" that happened back in 1865?

JEFFREY O'NEAL

Wait a minute, Patrick, you'll see
my point but, aren't you from South
Carolina?

PATRICK SULLIVAN

What? Ah yes. But what does
being from South Carolina have to
do with Deborah's lynching?

JEFFREY O'NEAL

You'll see, but, wasn't your home

town one of the southern states
featuring prewar restrictions to
negroes?

PATRICK SULLIVAN

I don't understand, but, yes, so
fucking what! Why must we keep
going back in the past, Jeffrey?

JEFFREY O'NEAL

Because, sometimes, Patrick, people
only learn to behave from what they
have been taught in the past.

PATRICK SULLIVAN

Then, Jeffrey, if you know all of
this, why are you harassing me?
don't know exactly what you're
looking for but, you're acting as
if your life is depending on it!

JEFFREY O'NEAL

Not just my life, Patrick, the
whole nucleus of mankind's
cultivation depends on our
relationship with one another in
America if we are to progress into
a successful society!

PATRICK SULLIVAN
(Looks up into the sky, shakes head side to side.)

Oh Lord, is this what this long
sermon's about.

(Stares back at Jeffrey.)

Okay, minister, what does living in
South Carolina have to do with the
lynching of Deborah Harris?

JEFFREY O'NEAL

Well, one the reasons, is because
of the 13th Amendment.

PATRICK SULLIVAN

And, if we're still talking about
the black codes, not just South
Carolina too, there were
regulations restricting the freedom
of Negroes to work in other places
too.

JEFFREY O'NEAL

Exactly, Patrick, and I don't think
the color of a person's skin should
infringe, or determine what to be
taught, or who should be taught!

PATRICK SULLIVAN
(Stares at Jeffrey a moment.)

You're really starting to worry me,
Jeffrey. Just what in the hell are
you talking about? The more I
listen to you, the more confused I
get!

JEFFREY O'NEAL
(Giggles.)

I guess Patrick, if you were the
principal of your own school,
Deborah Harris would have needed to
possess a one-thousand-dollar bond,
if she wanted to teach in your
school?

PATRICK SULLIVAN

Wait a minute, Jeffrey, am I
hearing you right? A thousand
dollar bond in guarantee of good
behavior. Is that what this
fucking head game is all about?

JEFFREY O'NEAL

Not exactly, Patrick, that's only
part of it. There's more to what
I'm trying to get you to see.

PATRICK SULLIVAN
(Smiles.)

Who the hell are you, a Civil War
buff? But if you insist professor,
the Black Codes also entitled
employers to whip Negro employees.
But you know, Jeffrey, I'm almost
afraid to ask you but, how does all
this tie in with the lynching of
Deborah Harris?

JEFFREY O'NEAL

Well, do you know where John
Johnson was born and raised before
he moved to Lexington, Alabama,
I've discovered?

PATRICK SULLIVAN

Well, from what I understand from
the gossip I heard at school, John
Johnson is from Tennessee. But
what does being from Tennessee have
to do with Deborah Harris's
lynching?

JEFFREY O'NEAL
(Giggles)

No, but listen, Patrick, and the KU
KLUX KLAN was also born in Pulaski,
Tennessee in 1865.

PATRICK SULLIVAN

On, the Ku Klux Klan were, so what?
But what does John Johnson, being
from Tennessee have to do with the
lynching?

(Suddenly surprised.)

Wait, Jeffrey, you're not trying to
imply that the principal is a Klan
member, are you?

JEFFREY O'NEAL
(Slowly shakes head, smiles.)

Yes, Patrick, John Johnson, I
believe is a Ku Klux Klan member!

PATRICK SULLIVAN
(Pause, stares at Jeffrey strangely.)

Jeffrey, you are starting to really
worry me. The principal, of all
people, would lynch Deborah Harris?
Do you know how bazaar that sounds,
Jeffrey?

JEFFREY O'NEAL
(Stares into space, slowly walks across the floor speaking.)

And, until this murder is solved, I
won't rest until justice is serve.

PATRICK SULLIVAN
(Interrupts, shouts.)

Until justice is served, Jeffrey,
what is your goddamn problem?
You're not the law, or a Negro!
what in hell's creation, you're so
worried about another lynching?
You better watch your ass, Jeffrey,
before they find you floating in
the river, face down, right next to
my white ass for starting such a
rumor.

JEFFREY O'NEAL
(Interrupts, slowly walks right up
In Patrick's face, stands.)

I have my reasons, Patrick. They
are the very same bastards who
raped, and killed my mother because
she had a Negro friend.

PATRICK SULLIVAN
(Interrupts, confused.)

But, Jeffrey, who in the hell are
we talking about? Well, I could
understand the Ku Klux Klan doing
it, but, the principal? Did you
actually witness the lynching
Jeffrey?

JEFFREY O'NEAL
(walks away from Patrick speaking.)

No, not exactly, Patrick, but, if a
person is taught to behave a
certain way from his or her past,
then the lynching of Deborah
Harris, makes John Johnson just as
guilty as the murder of my mother!

PATRICK SULLIVAN
(Giggles.)

Oh yeah, Jeffrey, but, I'm still
confused as shit! How does all
this tie in with John Johnson, if
he happens to be from Pulaski,
Tennessee?

JEFFREY O'NEAL
(Turns around at Patrick.)

Because, Patrick, in 1865 or maybe
early as 1865, who the fuck really
knows or cares, six veterans of the
confederate Army formed a secret
organization in Pulaski, Tennessee.

PATRICK SULLIVAN
(Interrupts, sighs.)

But, Jeffrey, excuse me for
interrupting but, that's only more
speculation. That's a pretty heavy
load to accuse someone of being a
murderer, Jeffrey. But, okay, I'll

meet you half way, and lets say I
did believe you, that still doesn't
prove your theory that John Johnson
lynched Deborah Harris.

JEFFREY O'NEAL
(Interrupts.)

But, didn't John Johnson used to
always tell you how he was going to
kill Deborah Harris, and he would
use any means necessary to get rid
of her, Patrick?

PATRICK SULLIVAN
(Chuckles.)

Yeah, ah, yeah, Jeffrey, ah, yeah,
but, ah, I didn't know telling you
any of this was going to effect you
that fucking much!

CHAPTER 3

EXT: EARLY MORNING - LIGHT RAIN - IN BED

Jeffrey and Betty Parnell lay in bed after making love all night. Preparing for his train ride to the busy metropolitan city of Pulaski, Tennessee. Jeffrey took extra care with the knotting of his tie in the bedroom mirror. betty's reflection in the mirror, sitting upright in the bed, topless, with the sheet pulled up to her waist, stares at Jeffrey, anticipating his meeting with John Johnson's parents. Jeffrey wanted an old-school integrity written across his personage in neat yet bold letters.

After kissing Betty good-bye, Jeffrey decides to drive his car instead of using the train to get to his destination. He drives his car by a circuitous route to avoid both the city traffic, and the backed-up highway traffic created from the construction work being performed on the new highway extension.

EXT: TWO WHITE MALES FOLLOWING IN A DARK VEHICLE

Also driving by the route behind Jeffrey's car was dark colored on with two white male figures inside. Jeffrey notices the car through his rear-view mirror but, he thought it was just another traveler on the same route as he, and continued his trip.

ANGLE ON: VISUALIZES THE LYNCHING OF DEBRA-GOES OFF ROAD

After Jeffrey finally gets back on the main extension to get to Pulaski, Tennessee, he visualizes Deborah Harris hanging from a tree again from her wrist in the nude. However, this time, Deborah's is not being whipped by a KU KLUX KLAN member. Her body just hangs from the tree slowly swinging back and forth from the blowing wind. No one else is around. The area is dark. Deborah's bloody clothes had been ripped off, and tossed over on some near by rock. Jeffrey can see Deborah's face clearly in his mind as the tears roll down her cheeks. Her eyes were badly swollen. Her head is titled upward from the tightness of the rope attached by the thick tree branch. Her face had been badly beaten.

Jeffrey had never seen Deborah's dead body after the actual lynching, but he could imagine the torment, pain, and the suffering she must have gone through. The thoughts of the lynching were so real in Jeffrey's mind, he could hear Deborah's voice pleading for help: "Jeffrey, help me please!" "Help me, Jeffrey!" "Jeffrey, help me please!"

THE VOICE IN JEFFREY'S MIND STARTED AT A LOW SOUND AND ENDED AT A HIGH SCREAM WHICH REVERBERATED THROUGH THE CAR/DEBORAH'S VOICE BECOMES SO LOUD, HE WAS UNAWARE THAT HE HAD DRIFTED THE CAR OVER INTO THE PATH OF THE ONCOMING TRAFFIC. JEFFREY SUDDENLY SNAPS OUT OF HIS TRANCE SECONDS BEFORE HITTING AN ONCOMING CAR IN HIS PATH. HE MANAGED TO SWERVE THE CAR OUT THE OTHER CARS PATH AND SKIDS INTO A DITCH ON THE SIDE OF THE ROAD. AFTER HITTING THE DITCH, HE SITS THERE WITH HEAD ON THE STEERING WHEEL. A SMALL CUT ON THE FOREHEAD, AND A LITTLE BLOOD STARTS TO FLOW FROM IT. JEFFREY TAKES OUT A HANDKERCHIEF AND WIPES AT IT. HE SAT THERE IN THE DITCH A MOMENT, TRYING TO PULL HIMSEF TOGETHER. SUDDENLY, A CAR ON THE HIGHWAY, WITH TINTED WINDOWS, SLAMS ON

IT'S BRAKES ALONG SIDE OF JEFFREY. HE QUICKLY LOOKS UP AT THE TINTED WINDOWS OF THE OTHER CAR, AND THE DRIVER SIDE WINDOW SLOWLY LOWERS, AND TWO PASSENGERS WEARING WHITE HOODED ROBES LAUGH HEARTILY AT HIM.

Jeffrey can't believe his eyes what he is seeing, so he shuts them tight and shakes his head, trying to clear his mind. However, when he open his eyes again, nobody is there on the highway. He sat there in the ditch a few more minutes until his nerves were calm, and then proceeded to drive his car out of the ditch. It took him three attempts before he was able to get out, and he speeds away back down on the highway, and thus, manages to arrive slightly ahead of schedule, just in time for breakfast.

It took Jeffrey a little than expected to find the home of Mr. and Mrs. John Johnson's in Pulaski, Tennessee. Outside of the Johnson home, in the car, Jeffrey sat. But before going to the door, he looked into his rearview mirror, and thought about his interlude with Betty. He saw Betty sitting in the bed just as he had left her before his trip, and remembered her saying:

BETTY

Honestly, Jeffrey Bradford, I think
it's real dumb to go all the way up
to Pulaski, Tennessee, a place
you've never been, because John
Johnson's parents telegram you to
pay them a visit about their son?
You don't know these damn people!

By the way, Jeffrey, Mr. Johnson is
a grown as man! What can his
parents possibly tell you about the
principal you don't know already?

JEFFREY O'NEAL
(Knotting tie in the mirror looking at Betty,
he heard himself say.)

But Betty, doesn't it seem mighty
strange that John Johnson
mysteriously disappears right
before the end of the semester, and
Deborah Harris was found lynched
from a tree?

Jeffrey was so deep into his thoughts that he didn't notice the SAME
DARK COLORED CAR with the two figures inside, pulling over to
the side of the road about a block away from his car.

A plump middle-aged woman, one Mary Johnson, and a plump
middle-aged man George Johnson, lived in a middle cklass sub urban
development in Pulaski, Tennessee, and preferred to start their day in
a leisurely fashion with a cup of coffee and one egg boiled precisely
three minutes, toast and strawberry preserves and cream cheese, three
strips of bacon fried crispy.

The bacon Mrs. Johnson cooked, had burned and the wind carried
the aroma out into Jeffrey's car. Jeffrey inhaled deeply, anticipated his
meeting, and jumps out of the car quickly, and goes up to the door
to knock. He raises his hand to knock on the door, but Mrs, Johnson
quickly swings it open:

MRS. JOHNSON

Good morning sir, how are doing
this morning? We didn't expect you
so early but, you're just in time]
for breakfast.

With a sinisterly grin, she opens the door wider for Jeffrey. Mrs. Johnson spun around quickly to go back into the kitchen, and motions for him to follow. Just as Jeffrey was about to step further inside the house, Mr. Johnson startles Jeffrey, who was sitting in a rocking chair, smiling sinisterly, slowly cleaning shotgun with a white cloth of some sort. Jeffrey froze in his tracks. He felt number. He couldn't speak. He just stood there, mouth opened, hands in the air.

GEORGE JOHNSON
(Slowly looks up at Jeffrey, interrupts.)

Well, boy, I've been waiting for
you since you left Lexington.

All of sudden, the tall grandfather clock in the corner of the living room chimes loudly.

Mrs. Johnson burst through the kitchen door towards Jeffrey carrying a knife. A loud fire engine truck alarm soar by the house. Mr. Johnson stood up and started walking towards Jeffrey with the shogun pointed at him. Jeffrey thought about Betty quickly when she said:

BETTY

I think it's real stupid of you,
Jeffrey Bradford, going all the way
to Pulaski Tennessee! You don't
know these people, and what they
might try to do to you."

As George Johnson got close to Jeffrey, he stuck out his hand to shake Jeffrey's, but Jeffrey shouted, "no," and quickly rushes out of the house and jumps back into his car. He tried to start the car, it stalled. He glanced over at the Johnson's home. George, with the shotgun, and Mary wit her knife, were coming down the front steps and towards the car. Jeffrey panics and tries to start the car, it stalls again.

INT. CAR. MORNING- JOHNSON'S APPROACHING WITH GUN

Jeffrey kept trying to start the car, jumping and down quickly from pushing on the gas pedal, it stalled. A shadow had cast over the front windshield from the morning light. Jeffrey looked up quickly and saw George Johnson's bloodshot eyes. The same bloodshot eyes hat John Johnson displayed back at the school in Lexington. The two shotgun circles were pressed up against the driver's side window. Jeffrey was terrified, he closed his eyes and started prying.

Moments pass, and Jeffrey calmed down when he didn't hear the blast of a shotgun. He slowly turned his head towards the driver side window and slowly opened his left eye. Then he quickly opened the right eye. Then he felt very embarrassed when he saw Mary and George Johnson, standing back away from the car with their arms around one another looking at him.

They were all back inside the kitchen, while Mary was finishing preparing the breakfast, George angrily looked Jeffrey up and down, then suddenly smiles and says:

GEORGE JOHNSON

Excuse me, sir, tell me something,
are all you folks up in Lexington,
Alabama as strange as you? What in
the hell you scream like some sissy
for, and then run out of the damn
house?

JEFFREY O'NEAL

But, I saw the shotgun, Mr.
Johnson, and the knife, and I
thought ah, ah, I thought you were
going to shoot me.

MARY JOHNSON
(Interrupts)

Oh, George, leave the young man
alone. We don't get many guest
around here anymore since our
little Johnny has gone to Lexington
to run the school. (Smiles.) How
would you like your eggs sir?

JEFFREY O'NEAL

Oh, ah, Mrs. Johnson, sunny side
up, thank you.

GEORGE JOHNSON
(Grins at Jeffrey)

But, sir, why would I shoot one of
us? Had you been one of those
Negro people pulling in front of
my property, I would have blown
your ass too short to shit!

MARY JOHNSON

Walks over in back of George, and places hands on his shoulders.

> But don't worry sir, George sits
> with his gun all day. You never
> know when those Niggers are going
> to start retaliating. But you can
> feel safe in out home as long as
> you're here.

GEORGE JOHNSON
(Slams table with first.)

> That's right, damn it! Ever since
> those niggers were set free, they
> think they can live anywhere they
> want to. but I'll be damn if they
> think they're gonna come on my
> property and destroy what I have.

MARY JOHNSON
(Smiles.)

> That's right, me and George are not
> going to do like all the rest of
> the neighbors have done, get scared
> and move to another area where no
> niggers can be found!

JEFFREY O'NEAL

> But wouldn't it be a lot easier and
> cheaper to stay on this property
> and learn to love one another?

GEORGE JOHNSON

Quickly pushes Mary's hands from his shoulders, and whips the Shotgun out from beneath the table and points it at Jeffrey.

> What did you say, son, live with,
> and love those niggers? Now, don't
> tell me a Nigger lover came all the
> way to Pulaski Tennessee to have
> his brains splattered all over Mrs.
> Mary Johnson's walls.

Jeffrey realizes that he had better be careful in what he said about the Negroes, and how he felt about them, if he wanted to get back to Lexington, alive. So, he chose his words accordingly.

JEFFREY O'NEAL
(Frowning, surprised.)

> Oh, ah, a Nigger lover, me? Hell
> no, I can't stand looking at those
> black, big lip, "cotton picking
> niggers!" Even if I had been a
> Nigger driving up on your property,
> Mr. Johnson, I wish you had a shot
> me, master!

(GEORGE JOHNSON)

(Smiles, slowly putting the shotgun back on his lap, Mary squeezes his shoulders gently.)

> Yeah, boy, if there's anything that
> bothers me more than a Negro, is a
> Nigger lover!

JEFFREY O'NEAL
(Sighs heavy)

Okay, but, Mr. Johnson, I'm
interested to know about your
little "Johnny boy" back in
Lexington, Alabama, High School.
Isn't that why I'm here?

GEORGE JOHNSON
(Looks at Mary, and trying
To ignore the question.)

Who, ah, my Johnny? Mary, fix this
nice young man some breakfast. How
would you like your eggs son?

MARY JOHNSON
(Smiles)

Er, sir, didn't you say, sunny side up?

JEFFREY O'NEAL
(Thinks himself as he speaks.)

Oh, ah, Mrs. Johnson, that's okay.
Don't go through any trouble. I've
eaten already anyway. No thank
you. I'm sorry.

GEORGE JOHNSON

What the hell are you sorry for?
if Mary and I had known what time
you were coming to Pulaski
Tennessee, we could have met you

at the dinner on the highway
extension. That would have saved
you five miles instead of driving
all the way out here to my home.

Mary Johnson spins around towards Jeffrey with his breakfast plate.
Hash browns, three strips of bacon, toast with butter and strawberry
preserves, and two sunny side up jumbo eggs.

JEFFREY O'NEAL
(Chuckles)

Wait a minute, Mr. Johnson, you and
Mrs. Johnson had no idea I was
coming to visit you? But, ah, the
letter you sent me. Didn't you
tell me in the letter to come any
time, I'm always welcome?

MARY JOHNSON
(Holding plate at breakfast, frowns at George)

Don't lie to him George. We knew
Mr. Bradford was coming to Pulaski
Tennessee.

GEORGE JOHNSON

Yeah, Mr. Bradford, we knew you
were coming but, I didn't know what
day or time. All Mary and I knew
was that they told us to be
prepared to have a stranger from
our little Johnny school up in
Lexington, Alabama, pay us a visit.

JEFFREY O'NEAL
(Surprised)

Ah, they? Ah, you and Ms. Johnson
knew all along I was coming but,
you didn't send me a letter telling
me to come and talk about Mr. John
Johnson, my boss at Lexington High
School. Your little "Johnny-boy".

But, but, how, sir? Ah, Mr.
Johnson, and you said, "they told
you and Mary to be prepared."
Who's they.

MARY JOHNSON
(Interrupts)

Walks up to Jeffrey reaching into her
apron, takes out a business card
Of some sort, and hands it to him.

Here, Mr. O'Neal, "they," are on
this business card they left us:

Jeffrey looked up a Mrs. Johnson, and at the card thrush in his face,
and slowly reaches for it with a shaking hand. He sits back in his seat
slowly reading the business card. slowly looks up at Mr. and Mrs.
Johnson and says.

JEFFREY O'NEAL
"The Federal Bureau of Investigation."

INT: DAY_WHIPS OUT SHOTGUN IN HIS FACE

GEORGE JOHNSON
(Whips out the shotgun and
points it at Jeffrey)

Who the hell are you boy? Are you
wanted by the law? I'll blow your
ass away from that fucking seat if
you don't tell me and Mary what the
hell you're doing here.

MARY JOHNSON
(Interrupts, gently pushes the front of the
shotgun away from Jeffrey.)

No, George, now you know we just
painted the kitchen walls. Let's
give Mr. O'Neal time to explain
himself.

GEORGE JOHNSON
(Quickly points a shotgun back at Jeffrey.)

Hell no, Mary, we could just paint
the damn kitchen again tomorrow,
but this man might be one of those
crazy bastards going around
killing, and cutting up people.
give yourself up son, you can't
run forever.

JEFFREY O'NEAL
(Frighten, hands in the air.)

But, Mr. Johnson, wait sir, don't
shoot me, please! Ah, remember,
(Holds up the card.) the FBI,
wants to talk to me alive.

Mr. Johnson angrily stares at Jeffrey for a moment still pointing
the shotgun at him. He looks over at the telephone hanging on the
kitchen wall near the entrance of the kitchen, then jerks his head
twice towards the phone.

Frustrated and confused, Jeffrey walks over to the phone, glanced at
the card, sighs, and dials the number. He briefly waits, patting his
right foot, shifting his weight from one leg to the other, before he
reaches someone on the other line, he speaks:

JEFFREY O'NEAL

"Hello, ah, to whom am
I speaking to sir?"
(Pause.)

"Yes, this is Jeffrey O'Neal!"
(Pause.)

"What sir?"
(Pause.)

"Of course, yes, but you should
know that!"
(Pause.)

"Yes, Lexington, High
School, in Alabama."

(Pause.)

"That's right sir!" (Pause.)
"Look, I don't like discussing a
personal friend's business to
strangers, and especially over the phone!"
(Pause.)

"I don't give a damn if you're the
FBI, the, CIA, or the fucking
President of the United States of
America,"

He quickly covers the mouth
receiver with his hand, and
whispers to Mrs. Johnson:

JEFFREY O'NEAL: OBSENCE? NOT, REALLY
PATRICK. WHAT'S SO OBSCENE ABOUT
TEACHING, AND SHOWIN HOW THE NEGROES
WERE, AND STILL ARE TREATED TODAY IN
WHITE AMERICA, TO HER WHITE STUDENTS?

Please forgive me for my language,
Mrs. Johnson.

MARY JOHNSON
(Nods in recognition smiles.)

I understand sir.

JEFFREY O'NEAL
(Places the phone back to his ear.)

"Excuse me sir, what?"
(Pause.) "Perjury!"

(Pause.)

"Fraud!"

(Pause.)

"A federal crime, but."

(Pause.)

"but sir, first of all,"

(Glances at the card in his hand.)

"someone drops off a little white card, and I'm just suppose to believe who the hell you say you really are?" "What, fine, then!" "Look, sir, that's besides the point!"

(Pause.)

"I have no more to say!"

(Pause.)

"That's right, I'll be here!"

(Pause, looks at the Johnson's.)

"Yes, that's all right with me."

I'm sure they would love to hear about it too."

(He slams the phone make on its base.)

After asking the Johnson's to be witnesses, Jeffrey sat on the patio outside of the kitchen waiting for the federal agents to arrive. Jeffrey, who never smoked, picked up an unlit cigarette and matches left in an ashtray on the table, lights it, and begins puffing on it, never inhaling. He suddenly realizes that he's a non-smoker, frowns, looks at the cigarette, then plucks it into the road. Jeffrey starts rocking his legs quickly side to side, looking around at his strange surroundings.

OS: TWO MALE VOICES FROM INSIDE KITCHEN

After hearing two male voices from inside the kitchen, Jeffrey freezes in his position, leans towards the kitchen screen door to listen, and to try and see who these persons were.

From the patio where Jeffrey was sitting, he could see a short, heavy-set white male in a black suit walk into the kitchen with George Johnson. Behind them, a tall thin Afro American male with broad shoulders wearing a navy-blue suit walked in afterwards. George pointed, without really looking towards the patio.

Everyone walks out into the patio, and Jeffrey quickly sits back as the agents flash their badges at him. Mary Johnson, smiling, brought out some plastic folding lawn chairs, and they all sat around one another. After settling down, the heavy-set agent extended his hand out to Jeffrey, and they shake hands, and the agent said:

AGENT STUMPY

Now, Mr. O'Neal, you have the
right to remain silent.

JEFFREY O'NEAL
(Flagging his hand, interrupts.)

Look, I know my rights and all that
crap, save your breath, ah, agent,
ah.

AGENT STUMPY
(Interrupts)

Agent Stumpy sir,
(points at the other agent.)

I'm sorry, its been a long day, and
my partner, Agent Robinson.

(Robinson nods.)

JEFFREY O'NEAL

Nods at Agent Robinson.

Hello sir.

AGENT STUMPY

(Looks at the Johnson's.)

> Now, Mr. and Mrs. Johnson, if you
> agree to sit out here with Mr.
> O'Neal's request, you may be called
> in to testify if any criminal
> charges are filed.

JEFFREY O'NEAL
(Stares up at Agent Robinson.)

> Excuse me, Agent Robinson, haven't
> I seen you in the principal's
> office at Lexington High School?

AGENT ROBINSON
(Glances at Agent Stumpy, hunches his shoulders.)

> No, sir, I don't believe you have.
> I don't remember ever seeing you
> until this case.

AGENT STUMPY

> Okay, Mr. O'Neal, my partner and I
> would like to know how close you

and Mr. Patrick Sullivan are? We
know you two at Lexington
High school together.

Jeffrey was caught off guard. He was surprise the agents mentioned
Patrick's name. His hands begins to shake. Suddenly, he is choke up
and struggling for breath. He wants to speak, but no words will come
out.

AGENT STUMPY

Come on, Mr. O'Neal we already know
about you and Patrick Sullivan's
childhood adventures down at the
lake with the Negro children.

Mary gasped and George Johnson's mouth and eyes stretched wide
open, and shocked at the very thought of a Nigger lover sitting outside of their home. Jeffrey's mind races with fear and indecision.

JEFFREY O'NEAL

Look, Agent Stumpy, I was just
trying to do what was right!
Deborah Harris was a dear friend of
me and Patrick. I had nothing to
do with the lynching if that's why
you and agent Robinson are hunting
me down for!

Jeffrey buries his face in his hands and sobs brokenly. Stumpy looks
at Agent Robinson and motions for him with his head to meet in
the corner of the patio away from everyone. he speaks softly and said

AGENT STUMPY

Look, Robinson, he's a pussy. I
thought he would put up a fight.
Let's take him away from here and
beat the "dog shit" out of him.
Maybe he'll talk then.

AGENT ROBINSON
(Stares at Jeffrey still sobbing,)

Yeah, Stumpy, I thought we would
have to put a fight too, but, we
can't be down here too much longer/
Let's get this shit over with and
get the out of here!

AGENT STUMPY
(Stares at Jeffrey still smiles.)

Okay, Robinson, but did you notice,
when I spoke about his childhood
with those, ah, ah, dark friends of
his, he broke down like a crying
baby!

AGENT ROBINSON

Look, I think we should take it
easy on him, Stumpy.

AGENT STUMPY
(Smiles at Jeffrey.)

He is finally breaking, Robinson, I
think he is about to talk. I know

we have to get back but, who else
would Deborah Harris have given it
to? She probably didn't trust
anyone else.

The two agents walk back over to Jeffrey. Agent Robinson walks around
in back of Jeffrey, gently grabs and squeezes his shoulders, and say:

AGENT ROBINSON
(Speaks in reassuring voice.)

Don't worry Mr. O'Neal just tell me
and agent Stumpy what you really
know about everything and we'll be
on our way.

JEFFREY O'NEAL
(Looks up over at Stumpy, watery eyes.)

Well, Agent Stumpy, Patrick
Sullivan had told me time and
again, that the principal was
planning to get rid of Deborah
Harris. I just thought it was, or
might have been the KU KLUX KLAN,
because of how she was murdered.

AGENT ROBINSON
(Walks back around in front of Jeffrey.)

But, Mr. Bradford, how can you be
sure if it really wasn't Mr.
Sullivan who was the actual killer?

JEFFREY O'NEAL

No, I don't think so. Patrick's not the murdering kind. Patrick Sullivan was just as much of a friend of Deborah Harris, as he is to me. Besides, Agent Robinson, I've even heard Mr. Johnson speak numerous times in front of me and Patrick, and I quote gentlemen: "That Black bitch can't come into my school and teach what the hell she wants to teach to my children. And if by the law, those, 'cotton picking educated Negroes, 'won't stop migrating into my school district, and if by the law those niggers are allowed to by the laws of the land, then gentlemen, I'll arrange to have it stopped my way, the confederate way," unquote, gentlemen.

AGENT ROBINSON
(Glances over at Stumpy, and they both raise their eyebrows at one another.)

But, Mr. O'Neal sir, according to
our investigation, isn't it true
that Mr. John Johnson had an affair
with the deceased. And if that is
the case, sir, then why would Mr.
Johnson lynched her then?

JEFFREY O'NEAL

Well, I don't know exactly. At one
time something was going around
about the principal and Deborah
Harris sneaking out together after
school, but, you know how rumors
are gentlemen, it may be true, it
may not.

(Smiles.)

AGENT STUMPY
(Glances at his watch, and up at Jeffrey.)

Let me ask you something Mr.
Bradford, the past school semester,
has Patrick or the principal ever
mention to you about a will Deborah
Harris made out to either Patrick
or John Johnson, or maybe even you?

JEFFREY O'NEAL
(Spins around at Agent Stumpy.)

Is this what this shit is all
about, a will? But, I thought it
was about the lynching?

AGENT ROBINSON

Excuse me, Mr. Bradford, just
answer the question!

JEFFREY O'NEAL
(Smiles.)

Well, gentlemen, I do believe
Deborah Harris had a will made out
before the school term ended. I
couldn't tell you personally to
who.

AGENT ROBINSON

Well, Mr. Bradford, right before
Deborah's death, $150,000 that she
had withdrawn from her bank account

is missing. And according to the
bank records, Deborah Harris had
promised not only to invest the
money in a trust fund for her
child's future education, but also
to match it with money she had
inherited from an elderly rich
white couple her mother used to
nurse.

JEFFREY O'NEAL
(Sighs heavy.)

Well, I'll be damn. You mean
Deborah was sitting on $150,000 all
that time. I'm shocked, gentlemen.
I never knew about that. But wait
a minute, you did say, her child's
future education? Was Deborah
Harris pregnant too? Then that
means there were two murders
committed, doesn't it?

(Giggles.)

AGENT STUMPY

Look, Mr. Bradford, whether it was
another murder committed or not,
that doesn't concern me and Agent
Robinson right now.

JEFFREY O'NEAL
(Chuckles)

Well, you boys can count me out on
that one. I'm absolutely sure if
Deborah was pregnant, it wasn't
mine. (Smiles.) Well, what
difference would it make now. They
both were murdered anyway!

AGENT ROBINSON

What are you talking about sir.
"they're both dead now," there was
only one death?

JEFFREY O'NEAL
(Snickers)

But doesn't I seem strange to you
agents that right before Deborah's
death, she would take out a life
insurance policy and have a will
made out. Shouldn't you two agents
be looking for a murderer instead
of harassing me?

AGENT ROBINSON

Listen, Mr. Bradford, the murder
investigation is being handled by
other agents. Agent Stumpy and I
are only interested in the money
withdrawn out of the bank before
Deborah's death.

JEFFREY O'NEAL
(Sighs heavy)

But that's what I keep telling you
two, sir, I don't know what in the
hell you agents are referring to.

AGENT STUMPY

(Interrupts, quickly snatches a briefcase up form under the table
where he's sitting, and takes out a few 100-dollar bills and thrush
them in Jeffrey's face.)

These Mr. O'Neal, me and Agent
Robinson would like to know if this
money looks familiar to you!

Jeffrey's eyes lights up, and he smiles seeing the money in Agent
Stumpy's hand, and digs out his wallet and pulls out three one hundred-dollar bills, and tossed them across the table at Stumpy, and say.

JEFFREY O'NEAL

There, damn it! If that's all you
and Agent Robinson wanted to know,
yes, that money in your hand does
look very familiar to me!

AGENT STUMPY

(Smiles, snatching the money from off the table starts checking
Jeffrey's money against some of the money from his brief case.)

See, Robinson, I told you it
shouldn't be too much longer now.

AGENT ROBINSON
(Sighs)

Yeah, I hope so, Stumpy, but how
does Mr. Bradford's money compares
to the serial numbers you have?

Stumpy vigorously, with a small magnify glass, checks several one
hundred-dollar bills from his brief case with Jeffrey's money lying on
the table. He narrows his eyes but keeps his anger to himself.

AGENT ROBINSON

Well, Stumpy, is there enough
proof? Shouldn't we be taken Mr.
Bradford back to Lexington Alabama
with us

AGENT STUMPY

Angrily stares at Jeffrey, holding his three one hundred-dollar bills in
his hand waving the money across Jeffrey's face.)

I thought you told me and Agent
Robinson, Mr. O'Neal, that this
money I have here in my brief case
looks familiar to you? Is this
some kind of joke, sir!

AGENT ROBINSON
(Steps forward.)

Now, Mr. O'Neal, if the money
doesn't look familiar to you, why
in the hell did you show us your
money then.

JEFFREY O'NEAL
(Angrily interrupts.)

Why sir! Why? I'll tell you and
that, (points at Agent Stumpy.)
"federal bastard," over there
checking my money as if I'm some
kind of common thief exactly why I
showed you my money. Because, damn
it, you asked me to show you,
didn't you.

AGENT STUMPY

Holding Jeffrey's money in his left hand waving it across the table in
Jeffrey's face, and the money from his briefcase in his other hand in
the sir, interrupts.

But, but, Mr. O'Neal, this money in
my left hand is not counterfeit.

JEFFREY O'NEAL
(Angrily snaps.)

I know damn well my money isn't
counterfeit too! How in the hell
am I suppose to know what you and
Agent Robinson were looking for?

CHAPTER 4

INT: FLAT ROAD: TWO LANE HIGHWAY NOTHING AHEAD BUT GAS STATION- CAR, MUSIC BY ELVIS ON A RAINY NIGHT

It has become the busiest and most popular of all the townships surrounding it. Running Creek was founded by the ancestors of the Honorable, Judge John hardy. Just beyond, on the access road to the new highway extension is Henry Pop Myers gas station. Henry had become a grandfather figure to most of the citizen of Running Creek County. He was well respected because of his long years of trusting, and reliable service to the community. Henry Pop Myers was one of the first country citizens who migrated to Running Creek County from Germany.

Due to vanity, Henry had imprudently heightened his visibility as a target. He was somewhat of a braggart and blabbermouth with casual acquaintances who frequently desire his service. At seventy years old, Henry stubbornly remained working alone at the gas station in search of his meager ration of social contact. He boasted about his profits to people and made it plain that he lived and worked alone.

EXT: MISTY EVENING- RAIN CAR PLAYING ELVIS PRESLEY

A car carrying two white teenagers, listening to Elvis Presley music, drive up slowly into Henry's gas station. They notice no once around and decides to walk up the steps which leads into Henry's office.

As the two teenagers quickly jump out of the car, their sneakers splashed into a puddle of muddy water around the station.

The two teenagers are different in many ways. One of them, Joey, has blonde hair and freckles, the other, James, has red hair and buck teeth, although they are different in features, their intentions are the same.

The evening sky was darker than usual. The teenagers look at one another and smile after discovering no one inside of the office after they entered. They both glance at the cash register on the counter along the wall in back of the office, and dash over to it. Upon reaching the cash register, they hear the toilet flush in the rear bathroom of the office, and they freeze in their tracks. Henry Pop Myers comes out of the office pulling up his zipper. His overalls are stained with oil and grease marks, and his face is smudged with dirt and grease too.

Henry looks up at the teenagers, startled, and say:

HENRY POP MYERS
(Smiling)

Oh, ah, gentlemen, excuse me, I'm
sorry, I didn't hear you come in.

(Points back at the bathroom)

You know, I keep meaning to fix
that toilet but, I get so busy
around here since the new highway
extension open, I don't have time
to get to the bank to deposit my
money.

The two teenagers' glance at each
other and smile, and glance back to
the open cash register.

HENRY POP MYERS
(Walks over to the picture of the ship on the wall.)

You know, gentlemen, have I ever
told you the story of my years of
service on my ship, the old, "Iron
General," me and my fellow service
men served on during the war?
The two teenagers' glance at each other
again and smile, and glance back
at the ship on the wall.

HENRY POP MYERS
(Sticks both of his hands out imitating guns, and loudly shouts)

"Boom, boom, boom," we used to
shoot those enemy airplanes down
like.

INT: ANOTHER_CAR APPROACHES STATION

A car horn blows loudly repeatedly from outside of the office. Henry
freezes, and looks through the window at a set of car headlights at the
gas pump outside, and smiles at the teenagers and say:

HENRY POP MYERS
(Smiles at the teenagers.)

Okay, gentlemen, stick around, I'll
be right back.

(He exits out of the office.)

The teenagers rush over to the open
cash register and discovers it has
no cash. James looks at Joey and says:

JAMES

Look Joey, I should of never let
you talk me into this. Let's get
the hell out of here before we get
in real trouble. The cash register
is empty!

JOEY
(Smiles.)

No, James, there's got to be some
money around here somewhere.
                    (Pushes James.)

Get out of here, and check the
window to see if that old bastard
is coming back!

JAMES
(Rushes over to look out of the window.)

No Joey, he's still outside
talking. Come on, lets get the
hell, out of here.

JOEY

Lifting the cash register's money tray, and pulling open the counter
drawers.

Fuck, James, there's not a damn
thing here!

JAMES
(Spins around from the window.)

See, that's why we should get the
fuck out of here before we get in
trouble, and maybe go to jail,
Joey!

JOEY
(Smiling, ignores James.)

This place is too busy since the
highway extension opened, James,
and you heard Henry Pop Myers tell
you himself, he can't get to the
bank. Henry must be hiding
the money from us.

JAMES
(Walks from the window.)

But why would Henry hide the money
from us, Joey, he wasn't expecting
us to rob him?

JOEY

Smiles, raising the front of his shirt from his pants, exposing the handle of a GUN tucked inside, pats it gently.

Well, if we can't find any money,
then I guess we'll have to persuade
Henry Pop Myers to tell us where he
hides it.

JAMES
(Freezes in disbelief shouts.)

What the fuck, Joey, a gun! You
never said anything about using a
gun. Where the hell did you get a
gun from?

JOEY

It doesn't matter where I got it
from! Just think of those innocent
people at war Henry Pop Myers
killed, and don't shout out my
name!

JAMES

No, Joey, that's a different kind
of killing. That was war. Henry
had permission!

JOEY
(Walks back and forth.)

Look, just relax James, the gun's
not loaded. I'm just going to
scare him, that's all.

JAMES
(SHOUTS.)

Damn it, Joey, if that was the
case, you could of used your
fucking finger to scare Henry!

JOEY
(Ignoring, James, walking back and forth.)

There's got to be some money around
here some place.

Suddenly the office door swings open and Henry walks in. The teenagers are facing one another arguing and Henry say:

HENRY POP MYERS

Okay, gentlemen, whose car is that
parked outside? It's starting to
get kind of busy.

JAMES

Ah, Mr. Myers, it's not my car,
sir. It belongs to Joey.

JOEY
(Spins around at James)

What the fuck you tell him my name
for, ass hole?

JAMES

Ah, ah, I don't know Joey, it
slipped out. This is a bad idea.
Let's get out of here!

HENRY POP MYERS

Look, James, it doesn't matter if
your friend tells me your name. I

need to know because your car is
blocking one of my gas pumps.

JOEY
(Quickly walks back and forth.)

Look, James, it's too late now. We
have to do it and get out of here
now!

HENRY POP MYERS

You boys are acting mighty strange.
come on, now, what can I help you
two with.

Another car horn blows repeatedly from outside of the office. Henry
looks through the office window and see two sets of car headlights at the gas pumps. As Henry spins around to exit, an old gray
hair woman, Mrs. Becker, comes in and bumps into Henry at the
entrance, and she said:

MRS. BECKER

Oh, Henry, talk about service, you
needn't know me down to serve me,
but, I need you to check something
in my car before this evening
services at church tonight.

HENRY POP MYERS
(Chuckles,)

Oh, I'm sorry, Mrs. Becker, but you
didn't have to get out in this
nasty weather to get me. I was

coming out. I was just talking to
James and Joey about their car
parked outside.

MRS. BECKER

(Turning her head to the side, exposing a hearing aid towards Henry.)

Yes, Henry I'm parked outside.
Can you look at my car for me
before I attend church this evening?

Henry gently grabs Mrs. Becker's
arm and as they slowly exit,
turns towards the teenagers and say:

HENRY POP MYERS

Now, you two gentlemen better make
up your minds what you want before
I get back, because I don't have
all day for your foolishness?

Joey walks out into the middle
of the floor and pace quickly
back and forth, and say:

JOEY

Look, James, I need some money
right away. I'm broke, and my
girlfriend's birthday is tomorrow.

JAMES
(Interrupts, shouts.)

A what? A fucking dress, Joey!
You're going to shoot and rob
someone over some pussy you'd
probably outgrow, and get tire of
in a month!

JOEY
(Spins around at James, pointing the gun at him.)

Look, you little bitch, stop
crying! If that's the way you
feel, you can walk your sissy ass
back to Running Creek County!

JAMES
(Hands in the air.)

Oh, that's the way it's going to
be, Joey! You're going to shoot me
now over some pussy that has you
climbing the walls. But, that's
all right, mother-fucker, you
better kill me, because I'll be on
your ass like flies on shit if I
live.

Henry Pop Myers had a slipped his way back into the office entrance watching the teenager's argue with one another, and he said:

HENRY POP MYERS

Reaching into his pocket, taking out a twenty-dollar bill, he extends his arm and money towards James.

Look, James, let's work something
out, here, you need money. Joey is
right, going to jail over something
stupid is crazy.

Joey stares at the twenty-dollar bill in Henry's hand, and then looks
at James and says:

JOEY

Can you believe this shit, James?
Where in the hell am I going to buy
a dress for twenty fucking dollars!

JAMES

I don't know Joey. But going to
jail for a damn dress isn't worth
it either! Just go to a damn five
and dime store. I sure you can buy
a couple of dresses for the bitch.

Henry Pop Myers tries to sneak to the front entrance while the
teenagers discuss the dress issue. As he steps the floor makes a loud
squeaking sound, he suddenly freezes, eyes tightly close, and Joey
spins around at him with the gun and said:

JOEY

Where are you sneaking off to, asshole?

JOEY UNLOADS HIS GUN, FIRING FIVE ROUNDS INTO
HENRY POP MYER'S BACK.

The force from the gunshot tosses Henry's frail body against the
entrance of the door, and he slams on to his back on the floor. James

rushes over to the dead body, stares briefly at it, and up, at Joey, and yells:

JAMES

What the fuck you had to shoot
Henry for? I think he's dead,
Joey! Now, what are we going to
do?

JOEY
(Smiles, and walks over to the dead body,
shoves James out of the way.)

Look, move the hell out of the way!
If you're gonna cry like some kind
of a bitch, go over in the fucking
corner.

(Joey searches through the dead body's pants pockets.)

There's got to be money somewhere.

SUDDENLY, A CAR HORN BLOWS REPEATEDLY FROM OUTSIDE OF THE OFFICE. JOEY AND JAMES GLANCE UP AT THE OFFICE FRONT WINDOW IT STARTS THUNDERING AND LIGHTNING AGAIN. THE CAR HORN BLOWS LOUDLY AND REPEATEDLY.

James looks down at Joey's open palm with fifty-five cents in it, shakes his head, and they dash out of the rear exit.

END OF SCENE

CHAPTER 5

EXT: NIGHT – DRIVING NEIGHBORS CAR ON E

LATER THAT SUNDAY NIGHT THE FETUS WAS READY TO PREVAIL, AND STARTED ITS JOURNEY THROUGH THE BIRTH CANAL. FREDERICK HARRIS WAS PREPARED. EARLIER HE HAD BORROWED A NEIGHBOR'S CAR. WHILE HE HELPED SADIE DOWN THE FRONT STEPS TO THE CAR, HE LOOKED AT HIS NEIGHBORS WINDOW, MRS. WHITE, WHO USUALLY IS LOOKING OUT OF HER WINDOW AT EVERYBODY AND EVERYTHING, THIS TIME HE ONLY SAW THE CURTAINS MOVE. AS SOON AS HE SAFELY GOT SADIE INTO THE CAR HE LOOKED AT MRS. WHITE'S WINDOW AND THERE SHE WAS LOOKING OUT THE WINDOW.

FREDERICK STARTED THE CAR, BUT IT STALLED, AGAIN HE TRIED AND IT STALLED. SADIE WAS MOANING AND IN PAIN- LABOR EVERY FEW MINUTES. MRS WHITE WAS WATCHING, AND VERY CONCERNED-KNOWING THEIR SITUATION. FINALLY, IT STARTED.

THE CAR IS ON "E".

FREDERICK APPROACHES HENRY POP MYER'S GAS PUMP BLOWING THE CAR HORN REPEATEDLY. FREDERICK BECOMES VERY ANGERY WHEN NO ONE COMES OUT TO PUMP GAS. HE LOOKS AROUND THE STATION WONDERING WHERE ANYONE IS. FREDERICK LOOKS

AT THE FOOTPRINTS IN THE MUD FILLED WITH WATER FROM THE PREVIOUS RAINS, BUT DOESN'T NOTICE THE COUNTY SHERIFF'S CAR WITH TWO OFFICERS SITTING INSIDE WATCHING HIS EVERY MOVE A SHORT DISTANCE AWAY.

SADIE HARRIS:
(slowly rocking back and forth)

Fred, where are we? Why are you
stopping the car? Are we at the
hospital yet?

FREDERICK HARRIS:

QUICKLY LOOKING AROUND AT THE STATION, HE POUNDS ON THE HORN AGAIN.

Not yet, Sadie, I'll get you to the
hospital. I need some gas. I
don't know what's wrong with the
gas needle, but I thought I had
enough gas to get across the
county.

SADIE HARRIS:
(holding stomach in pain, moaning)

Oh, Fred, let's go honey! We can't sit here.

Fred leaps out of the car into the
mud and rushes into the
gas station. Fred charged into
the door and immediately
trips over Henry's bloody body.
He is covered with blood

from falling on him. Sadie pounds
on the car horn and Fred
runs over to the office window
and peeps out at her, and
suddenly notices the sheriff's car
parked in a distance but,
they are no longer sitting inside of the car.

Fred suddenly spins around
in shock, in disbelief. He
notices the cash drawer open-
the dead body with pockets
turned inside out. Sadie pounds
on the car horn again. But
as soon as Fred decides to run
out of the front office
entrance he bumps right into the
two sheriffs who were out
sitting in the car watching him.

FREDERICK HARRIS:

STANDING IN FRONT OF THE TWO SHERIFFS' COVERED
IN BLOOD PLEADING:

Oh, thank you sir, you're just in
time. I have to get to the
hospital as soon as possible.

THE TWO SHERIFFS' JIMMY JOMES, AND ANDY SMITH
QUICKLY LOOK AT FRED UP AND DOWN, THE DEAD
BODY AND THE OPEN CASH REGISTER AND JIMMY
JONES IMMEDIATELY HITS FRED OVER THE HEAD WITH
HIS BLACK JACK. FRED FALLS TO THE FLOOR WITH
A BLOODY OPEN WOUND ON THE TOP OF HIS HEAD.
AFTER FALLING TO THE FLOOR, THE SHERIFFS BEGIN

KICKING HIM REPEATEDLY SCREAMING OBSCENITIES. DEPUTY SMITH GRABS FRED'S HEAD BACKWARDS BY THE HAIR STICKS THE REVOLVER IN FREDS MOUTH AND COCKS THE HAMMER.

DEPUTY JONES:

(interrupts- quickly pulls
deputy smiths' arms with
the gun away from fred's
mouth)

NO ANDY- NOT HERE. FIRST WE NEED A SUSPECT TIE HENRY POP'S MURDER UP, THEN WE'LL KILL HIM.

SUDDENLY, SADIE WOBBLES SLOWLY INTO THE OFFICE HOLDING HER STOMACH WITH ONE HAND – IN THE OTHER SHE'S POINTING A SMALL REVOLVER AT DEPUTY JONES STANDING OVER FRED'S BLEEDING FACE AND HEAD AND SHOUTS:

(oh, God what are you
doing to my husband?)
(she drops to her knees
grabbing her stomach and
drops the gun)

SUDDENLY DEPUTY SMITH LEAPS OUT BEHIND SADIE AND SMASHED HER OVER THE HEAD WITH HIS BLACK JACK. SHE FELL TO THE FLOOR NEAR FRED, THE DEPUTIES BEGAN TO VICIOUSLY KICKING HER

STANDING IN FRONT OF THE TWO SHERIFFS' COVERED IN BLOOD, PLEADING:

Oh, thank you sir, you're just in

Time. I have to get to the
Hospital as soon as possible.

THE TWO SHERIFFS' JIMMY JONES, AND ANDY SMITH
QUICKLY LOOK AT FRED UP AND DOWN, THE DEAD
BODY AND THE OPEN CASH REGISTER AND JIMMY
JONES IMMEDIATELY HITS FRED OVER THE HEAD WITH
HIS BLACK JACK. FRED FALLS TO THE FLOOR WITH
A BLOODY OPEN WOUND ON THE TOP OF HIS HEAD.
AFTER FALLING TO THE FLOOR, THE SHERIFFS BEGIN
KICKING HIM REPEATEDLY SCREAMING OBSCENITIES.
DEPUTY SMITH GRABS FRED'S HEAD BACKWARDS BY
THE HAIR STICKS THER REVOLVER IN FREDS MOUTH
AND COCKS THE HAMMER.

> DEPUTY JONES:
> (interrupts- quickly pulls
> Deputy smith;s arm with
> The gun away from fred's
> Mouth)

NO ANDY- NOT HERE. FIRST WE NEED A SUSPECT TIE
HENRY POP'S MURDER UP, THEN WE'LL KILL HIM.

SUDDENLY, SADIE WOBBLS SLOWLY INTO THE OFFICE
HOLDING HER STOMACH WITH ONE HAND- IN THE
OTHER SHE'S POINTING A SMALL REVOLVER AT DEPUTY
JONES STANDING OVER FRED'S BLEEDING FACE AND
HEAD AND SHOUTS:

> (oh, God what are you
> Doing to my husband?)
> (she drops to her knees
> Grabbing her stomach and
> drops the gun)

SUDDENLY DEPUTY SMITH LEAPS OUT BEHIND SADIE AND SMASHED HER OVER THE HEAD WITH HIS BLACK JACK. SHE FELL TO THE FLOOR NEAR FRED, THE DEPUTIES BEGAN TO VICIOUSLY KICKING HER.

CHAPTER 6

EXT: COURT ROOM

JUDGE HARDY:

Will the two attorneys please
identify themselves:

JAMES O'CONNOR:

QUICKLY STANDS UP AND SHOUTS

The people versus the defendants
James O'Connor, present Your Honor

ROBERT M. MORRIS:

SLOWLY SLIDES CHAIR BACK AND STANDS

Robert M. Morris, present Your
Honor, representing and defendants
Mr. Frederick and Sadie Harris.

The Stenographer- old fashioned white lady- sits in court-room
operating keys.

JAMES O'CONNOR:
(smiles)

Good morning, ladies and gentlemen
of the jury, August 4th 1956 it
rained practically each day and
night the whole weekend. Also, that
same evening, the defendants
Frederick Harris and Sadie Harris,
decided it was an excellent time to
commit a murder and robbery.

JAMES O'CONNOR TURNS AND FACES THE JUDGE AND
GIVES HIM A LOOK OF ASTINISHMENT. SUDDENLY
REALIZES THAT THE WEATHER CONDITIONS WERE
ANOTHER MOTIVE HE COULD USE TO HELP WITH
THE PROSECUTION. THE JUDGE GRINS A LITTLE BUT
DOESN'T SHOW HIS TEETH.

The judge nods his head a little slowly at O'Connor.

O'Connor proceeds to face the jury.

ROBERT M. MORRIS:
(INTERRUPTION-stands up)

Objection, Your Honor! Mr. O'Connor is misleading the jury. The
defendants haven't been found guilty or innocent.

JEFFREY O'NEAL

(Sir, I'm merely stating
the circumstances)

ROBERT M. MORRIS:

Your Honor how can the prosecutor
use the weather as a circumstance?

JUDGE HARDY:

Overruled, Mr. Morris!

JAMES P'CONNOR:

Thank you, Your Honor!

TURNS BACK TOWARD THE JURY

Ladies and Gentlemen of the jury,
the defendant couldn't have chosen
a better time of day to commit the
crime. Nobody at around, church,
raining- neighbors in the house

ROBERT M. MORRIS:

Objection, Your Honor, the defendants never confessed to any such
crime. Mr. O'Connor can't put words in Mr. Frederick's or Sadie's
Harris's mouth or read their minds.

JUDGE HARDY:

Overruled, Mr. Morris!

ROBERT M. MORRIS:

If Fred and Sadie knew this was a
perfect time to commit the crime
why didn't they see anyone? The

first thing they should have done
was sit and wait until the coast
was clear?

ROBERT MORRIS: CATCHES HIMSELF. SHAKS HIS HEAD
AND PULLS HIMSELF TOGETHER BECAUSE HE STARTED
TO BELIEVE WHAT THE PROSECUTOR WAS TRYING TO
GET THE JURY TO BELIEVE- HE SHOUTED

ROBERT M. MORRIS:

Objection, your honor the defendant's neighbor Mrs. White is called
to the witness stand. Her huge breast is squeezed tightly together in
her low-cut black blouse she wore.

MRS. WHITE:

I hope this is the last time you
and James drag me down here sonny?
You send those deputies to my house
they speed down the highway getting
me here. We can end this right
now, the colored couple should be
free. Just leave them out of
Henry's murder. The boy was taking
his wife to the hospital to have a
baby- why the hell would he rob
someone?

JUDGE HARDY:

(Interrupts, slams the gavel Mrs. White jumps)

Order in the court, Mrs. White!
First of all, name, I'm to be
addressed as, Your Honor, and

second, you're only up here to
prosecute, ah ah I meant to be a
witness

Points the gavel near her face.

MRS. WHITE:

Slowly pushes the gavel away.
Look, sonny, this wooden hammer is
to be used on that wooden saucer in
front of you, and not in my face.

JUDGE HARDY:

HE RISES SLOWLY, THE CHAIR SLIDES BACKWARDS
CAUSING A SCREECHING SOUND. HE WALKS OVER TO
MRS. WHITE

Mrs. White is it true you live
across the road from the murderers.

ROBERT M. MORRIS:

OBJECTION YOUR HONOR, THE DEFENDANTS ARE NOT
TO BE CONSIDERED MURDERERS BY THE PROSECUTORS
UNTIL THEY'RE FOUND GUILTY!

JUDGE HARDY:
(SMILES)

Objection Sustained! Mr. O'Connor
you're not to make any such remarks
again, understand

JAMES O'CONNOR:
(smiles)

Of course, Your Honor

SPINS AROUND TO THE JURY

Okay. Ladies and Gentlemen of the
jury, let me put it a different
way.

TURNS TO MRS. WHITE

Now Mrs. White, is it true you live
cross the road from the
defendants?

MRS. WHITE:
(Stares strangely at O'Connor).

What kind of crazy question, James
you've known where I've lived ever
since you were knee high to a fire
hydrant.

JUDGE HARDY:
(Interrupts and slams the gavel- Mrs. White jumps)

Just answer the question, Mrs.
White, we don't need to know the
prosecutors' story.

MRS. WHITE:
(Grabs both ears with each hand)

Well, maybe if you stop hitting
that wooden saucer with that wooden
hammer I could hear clearly.

THE JURY AND SPECTATORS GIGGLE LOUDLY.

JUDGE HARDY:
(Looks at the giggling faces and over at
Morris smiling, he slams the gavel hard five
times and shouts)

Order- everyone, order! Order in
the court!

MRS. WHITE:
(look into her purse and takes some tissues
out and places in front of the judge)

Here, sir lay these tissues on top
of that wooden saucer so the next
time you hit it- it won't make me
jump!

The jury and spectators giggle loudly.

JUDGE HARDY:

ORDER! ORDER!

CHAPTER 7

DURING THE RECESS OF THE TRIAL, IN THE JUDGE'S CHAMBER, JUDGE HARDY SPEAKS PRIVATELY WITH THE PROSECUTOR, MR. JAMES O'CONNOR, AND THE LAB TECHNICIAN ABOUT THE EVIDENCE OF THE CRIME FROM THE MURGER OF THE HENRY POP MYER'S CASE. THE JUDGE IS SITTING BEHIND HIS HUGE MAHOGANY DESK, WHILE THE OTHER TWO ARE STANDING IN FRONT OF HIS DESK WITH TWO SOFTS CUSHIONED GREEN CHIARS PLACED BEHIND THEM.

JUDGE HARDY

Okay gentlemen, now let's get to
the bottom on this case. The trial
could go on for another hour or
two. We know the Harris defendants
Are guilty of murdering Henry Pop
Myers. I'm absolutely sure this
murder couldn't have been committed
by no one else but those colored
people.

JAMES O'CONNOR
(Smiles at the crime lab technician.)

That's true, Your Honor, and let's
not forget about the robbery too.

JUDGE HARDY

Oh, yeah, O'Connor, that's right.
I'm so rapped up with the murder, I
wasn't even thinking about the
robbery.

TECHNICIAN

Excuse me, Your Honor, but my team
and I searched the entire crime
scene and discovered enough
evidence to prosecute who ever
committed the murder and robbery
too.

JUDGE HARDY
(Chuckles.)

Do you hear what I'm hearing,
O'Connor? He said," whomever
committed the murder and robbery,"
as if we don't have the real
suspects already in custody.

JAMES O'CONNOR
(Smiles.)

I hear you, Your Honor, but, I
don't know exactly what the crime
lab technician is referring to.

TECHNICIAN
(Steps forward.)

Look, Your Honor, sir, I know you
and the prosecutor is optimistic
about the possibility of the Harris
couple being guilty but.

JUDGE HARDY
(Interrupts, and shouts.)

Damn it, sir, and that's right!
It's been a couple of years since a
murder and robbery have been
committed in Running Creek County,
Alabama, and the finding them guilty
will let the county citizens know
that they can sleep peacefully that
a murderer is behind bars.

JAMES O'CONNOR
(Steps forward next to the technician, and smiles.)

So, sir, you're wasting your time
here searching for answers. We
already know who the real murderers
are!

JUDGE HARDY
(Pointing his finger at the technician.)

Let me tell you something boy!
Now, I'm not saying we're perfect
in Running Creek County. Of
course, we had our share of
problems but, since those niggers

have been moving into our county,
the neighbors are afraid to come
out of their home.

TECHNICIAN

Well, Your Honor, I wasn't aware of
this but, I don't see why. Maybe
if the neighbors knew the truth,
ah, they wouldn't be afraid to
socialize with one another.

JUDGE HARDY
(Leans forward towards technician.)

That's exactly one of the problems,
sir! When my great-grandfather was
the salve master of the Running
Creek Plantation, they were able to
keep them colored people in
control. The county neighbors
weren't afraid to come out of them
homes!

TECHNICIAN
(Thinks to himself a moment.)

Interesting, Your Honor, very
interesting in deed. But, Your
Honor, I would just like to show
you and Mr. O'Connor something our
crime lab discovered which will
probably startle the both of you.

JUDGE HARDY
(Chuckles, looks at O'Connor, and sits back in seat.)

Well, sir, the floor is yours.
what do you have that's so
interesting to show Mr. O'Connor
and I?

JAMES O'CONNOR
(Sits down in the chair behind him and crosses his leg.)

I don't know what the crime lab
might have found any different then
what we have already, Your Honor,
but, I'm interested to know too
sir.

TECHNICIAN
(Slowly looks at the Judge and prosecutor, sighs, then walks over to

the corner of the room and sets up an
easel with blown up photographs
of three sets of fingerprints on it.)

Your honor, sir, me and my staff
have found these fingerprints all
the crime scene.

JAMES O'CONNOR
(Smiles at the Judge.)

That's great, Your Honor, now we
have more evidence to prosecute the
defendants.

JUDGE HARDY
(Smiles, wipes forehead with a handkerchief.)

You see, James, I told you not to
worry about anything. I'm the
Judge of Running Creek County, and
we'll prosecute to the fullest
extent of the law.

JAMES O'CONNOR
(Suddenly stands, and stares at the prints,
and looks at the Judge, and
walks quickly over to the prints.)

Wait, Your Honor, these are three
different sets of prints. But the
sheriff and deputies said there
were only two suspects at the crime
scene.

JUDGE HARDY
(Giggles.)

Hey James, maybe that third print
belong to that missing colored
child that deputies couldn't find at
the crime scene. Maybe the child
escaped

TECHNICIAN

Excuse me, Your Honor, but whether
a third suspect was present at the
scene or not, remains to be seen.
We weren't able to find the colored
defendant's prints at the crime

scene at all. We searched the
entire gas station sir, and none.

JUDGE HARDY
(Stands, and leans forward across his desk
towards the technician, and shouts.)

Just what the hell do you mean, you
weren't able to find the colored
defendant's prints at the murder
scene? The damn Deputies caught
the colored boy standing over Henry
Pop Myers' dead body lying on the
floor, and he had Henry's blood all
over his body!

JAMES O'CONNOR
(Quickly turns at the technician and shouts.)

But, sir, the defendant's
fingerprints had to have been at
the crime scene! You've even seen
the Deputies sworn statement
yourself, which clearly verify the
Nigger murdered the victim in cold
blood!

TECHNICIAN
(Hunches shoulders.)

Well, Mr. O'Connor, whether Mr.
Harris murdered Mr. Myers or not,
doesn't concern me. My job is just
to find prints. Now, whether the
prints coincide with the murder,
that's the problem of the District

Attorney's office, not mine!

JUDGE HARDY
(Flops back in his seat, and stares at the prints for a moment.)

O'Connor, just who in the hell is
this young Public Defender? Jus
where did the fuck he come from!

JAMES O'CONNOR
(Walks over to the Judge's desk.)

Well, sir, from my sources, Mr.
Morris is from the other side of
Running Creek County. He's within
his jurisdiction, Your Honor.
Also, the word from the office is,
Mr. Morris is supposed to be some
kind of colored crusader of justice
for the Negroes. And get this,
Your Honor, Mr. Morris claims this
American law system has noble
ideals, but, are ignored in
practice by the law which serves
the white communities only.

JUDGE HARDY

Now do you see what I mean,
O'Connor. Just because those
colored folks don't want to pick
cotton anymore for us, they think
they can come down here in me
forefather's land to rob and
murder. Now the bastards are
defending one another, O'Connor!

JAMES O'CONNOR
(Chuckles.)

Yeah, I know, but, Your Honor,
you're the Judge. You can make the
final decision.

JUDGE HARDY
(Leans forward, points his finger at the technician.)

Now, son, I'm the Judge, and I'll
make the final decisions in Running
Creek County. So, if you know any
better, those colored people print
better start showing up! I'm quite
sure, your superiors recommended you
to help me out with this case,
true?

TECHNICIAN
(Looks at O'Connor, and the Judge's frowning faces.)

Yes, Your Honor, that is true, but,
why are you and the prosecutor
fighting me? My job consists of
finding evidence. I'm only
presenting these facts to you and
Mr. O'Connor, so you're able to
straighten things out with the
prosecution, sir.

JUDGE HARDY
(Sits back and smiles at O'Connor)

You know, O'Connor, the lab
technician reminds me of Joey a

little bit. All he needs is blonde
hair, and you'd probably think they
were brothers.

TECHNICIAN
(Quickly looks up at the Judge, eyebrows rise.)

Ah, Joey with the blonde hair, Your
Honor, who's he, sir?

JUDGE HARDY
(Giggles.)

Ah, Joey is my brother's son who
was up visiting us this past
summer, why?

TECHNICIAN
(Sighs, grins at O'Connor.)

I bet too, Your Honor, Joey is the
only teenager with blonde hair
visiting, or lives in Running Creek
County, Alabama, with blonde hair
this past summer?

JUDGE HARDY
(Quickly sits forward glances at O'Connor.)

Ah, yes, but ah, the neighbors and
I always thought that was strange
but, you had to be living around
Running Creek County to realize
this.

O'Connor hunches his shoulders at the Judge.

TECHNICIAN

Well, Your Honor, during our crime
scene dusting for prints, the
defendant's fingerprints were no
where to be found. What we did
find strange Your Honor, were the
red and blonde hair fibers at the
crime scene.

JUDGE HARDY
(Leaps up, leans forward across the desk.)

Just what the hell are you
insinuating, sir, that the suspect
has red hair?

JAMES O'CONNOR
(Quickly sits in the chair next to the technician.)

But that's impossible. I've rea
the arrest report, and the Deputies
never said that Joey was at the
scene, nor a red hair suspect either.

TECHNICIAN
(Looks at O'Connor.)

Look, Mr. O'Connor, I'm not
interested in what the Deputies
said in their arrest report, or
Joey, and this possible other red
hair suspect if that is the case.
As I said before, that's your
problem. I'm only here to find
prints only.

JUDGE HARDY
(Slowly sits back in his seat, frowns at O'Connor.)

I just don't understand where this
case is going, O'Connor. I thought
when the defendants were caught at
the crime scene, no other suspects
were involved.

TECHNICIAN
(Walks over in front of the Judge's desk.)

Excuse me, Your Honor, but I think
I have an idea exactly where this
case is heading, sir.

JUDGE HARDY
(Snickers, glances at O'Connor.)

Oh, you do, sir. Why don't you
tell Mr. O'Connor and I where the
case is going.

TECHNICIAN

Look, I'm not a doctor or a lawyer,
but I heard from a reliable source
that this Negro crime fighter is
out to charge Running Creek County
Sheriff's office with murder.

JAMES O'CONNOR
(Laughs at the technician.)

What did you say sir, murder? How
in the hell is Mr. Morris going to

charge Running Creek County with murder when only one murder was committed?

TECHNICIAN
(Holding up his hands.)

Wait, don't shoot me. But from what I understand, Mr. O'Connor, Mr. Harris was on his way taking his wife to the hospital. Mrs. Harris was about to deliver their first child. I'm sure it's in your records, Mr. O'Connor.

JAMES O'CONNOR
(Sighs, frowns.)

Yes, I know, I saw it! And I still can't figure out how the Public Defender is going to prove that an unborn child should have the same jurisdiction as a human being.

JUDGE HARDY
(Shouts.)

Non-sense, the only murder committed was by the defendants caught at Henry Myers' gas station, damn it!

TECHNICIAN
(Quickly looks at O'Connor and the Judge, shouts.)

Hey, don't chew me the hell up!
Have you gentlemen ever considered
the deputies murdering the fetus
when they apprehended the
defendants at the murder scene?

JAMES O'CONNOR
(Stares at the technician.)

How in the hell can someone be
charge with murder for something
that's no even human yet?

TECHNICIAN

Well, Mr. O'Connor, that's a matter
of opinion. Buy if you ask me my
personal feelings, the Harris fetus
was about to be born. The fetus
was moving, kicking, fighting for
it's survival. When the breathing
stops, Mr. O'Connor, that is when
death occurs.

JAMES O'CONNOR
(Snickers.)

Well I'll be damn, sir, next thing
you'll be telling the Judge and I,
if I go our into the courtyard's
garden and cut some flowers from
their stems, they will stop
breathing too!

TECHNICIAN
(Smiles at O'Connor.)

Why, yes, you do have a good point
there, Mr. O'Connor. Every form of
life has the basic origin of life,
DNA

JAMES O'CONNOR
(Chuckles.)

Oh, yeah, is that true! So the
next time I'm home gardening, and
pull some plants from by backyard,
you can have been arrested for murder
too!

JUDGE HARDY
(Worried looking.)

No, O'Connor, he does have a good
point there. I personally never
looked at life in that form, but if
the jury looks at life that way, it
could change the whole outcome of
the verdict.

JAMES O'CONNOR
(Giggles.)

Be for real, Your Honor, do you
really think the jury would
jeopardize Running Creek County's
reputation over a fetus?

JUDGE HARDY

But just say for example, O'Connor,
if the jury see life that way.
That means the blonde hair, or the
red hair suspect, could be
responsible for Henry Pop Myers'
murder!

JAMES O'CONNOR
(Smiles, winks his eye at the Judge.)

Or, Your Honor, to be on the safe
side, what if the defendants are
persuaded to testify and plead
guilty.

END OF SCENE

CHAPTER 8

EVERYONE IS BACK INSIDE THE COURTROOM DURING ROBERT M. MORRIS'S ARGUMENT. ROBERT BROUGHT AN EASEL AND BLOWN UP PHOTOGRAPHS OF UNBORN, AND ABORTED CHILDREN, TO PROVE HIS THEORY THAT THE HARRIS FETUS WAS, OR SHOULD BE CONSIDERED A HUMAN BEING BY THE JURORS.

ROBERT M. MORRIS
(Sets up the easel with a blown-up picture of a
fetus in view of the jurors and Judge.)

Your Honor, sir, and ladies and
gentlemen of the jury, I have here
on this easel I brought in court
today, is a photograph of a
developing fetus at ten weeks old.
As everyone can plainly see,

CU: EASEL IN THE COURTROOM

(-ROBERT POINTS OUT AND COUNTS-)

a fetus at his very minute existence has, or had, hands, fingers, and toes, just like me, you, and like any average child running and playing out in the park.

JUDGE HARDY
(Leans forward, glances at the prosecutor, and back
at the photograph to get a closer view.)

Excuse me, Mr. Morris, how did you
manage to get this photograph of
this flesh, ah, ah, er, this thing.
Is it still alive?

ROBERT M. MORRIS
(Spins around to the jurors.)

Ladies and gentlemen of the jury,
on this easel right in front of
your eyes are an actual photograph
of a fetus which has been blown up
ten times its original size.

JUDGE HARDY
(Glances at the prosecutor who hunch his
Shoulders at the Judge, interrupts.)

Okay, okay, counselor, we
understand. But, what I would like
to know, is this thing still alive
today.

ROBERT M. MORRIS
Walks over and stands in front of the Judge,
and spins around at the jurors.

Unfortunately, not, your honor, and
ladies and gentlemen of the jury,
no! This is actually what's left
of a developing child of ten weeks
after it was murdered.

JUDGE HARDY
Glances at the prosecutor who raises his eyebrows back at the Judge.

Look, Mr. Morris, how could that
be felonious, counselor? Tell the
court how this, "flesh," should
have the same rights as a child,
"running in the park,' as you
claimed earlier.

ROBERT M. MORRIS
(Quickly walks over in front of the jurors,
pointing back at the photograph.)

But, look carefully over at the
photograph, ladies and gentlemen of
the jury. That's what's left of a
developing unborn child, with ten
fingers and toes, just like you and
I have, looks like when it's killed
by suction abortion.

JUDGE HARDY
(Glances at the photograph, and back at Robert, interrupts.)

And you want the court to bring
felony charges on this thing,
counselor? A bunch of flesh!
(Looks back over at the
photograph a moment.)

By the way, I only see one foot on
that photograph. Where's the other
foot counselor?
(Snickers.)

Don't tell us this is a handicapped
fetus.
(The court spectators and jury giggles.)

ROBERT M. MORRIS
(Walks over to the Judge.)

I'm glad you asked that question,
Your Honor.

Replaces the photograph on the
easel with another one of the
same fetus held in a human
hand showing its feet.

No, Your Honor, this is not a
handicapped child, but,

(Spins around at the jurors.)

ladies and gentlemen of the jury, I
just replaced the other photograph
with that same fetus being carried
by the human hand

JUDGE HARDY
(Glances at the prosecutor who's looking at
the photograph himself, and the
Judge leans forward looking back at the photograph, interrupts.)

Are those little feet in that
person's hands, counselor?

ROBERT M. MORRIS
(Walks over to the jurors, steps aside
and points at the photograph.)

Yes, Your Honor, and ladies and
gentlemen of the jury, tiny little
human feet. And if you observe
closely, those are miniature feet
with ten miniature toes to go along
too. And that, ladies and
gentlemen of the jury, is what your
feet looked like when you were ten
weeks old.

JUDGE HARDY
(The court room's silent. He
stares at the photograph a moment,
and up at the prosecutor who's
writing something down on paper,
interrupts.)

Oh, really counselor, very interesting.

ROBERT M. MORRIS
(Walk's over to the Jude, interrupts.)

Very interested indeed, sir.

(Points towards the photograph.)

That child's feet on that
photograph, Your Honor, I'm showing
you and the jury,

(Spins towards the jury.)

They are perfectly formed just like
mine, yours, the prosecutor, and
yours, ladies and gentlemen of the
jury also.

JUDGE HARDY
(Looks over at the prosecutor who's reading some material from his
Table, and back at Robert.)

Well, counselor, I guess next
you'll tell the jury this thing had
fingerprints too.

ROBERT M. MORRIS
(Walks back over to the jury, and points
back over to the photograph.)

Yes, ladies and gentlemen of the
jury, that fetus small hand over
there on that photograph has, or
had fingerprints too. No, if
anyone of you jurors could show me
A human being without any
fingerprints, I'll be glad to show
you a zebra without stripes.

JUDGE HARDY
(Slowly sits back into his chair, sighs, and rub eyes.)

No, no, no, Mr. Morris, this is
nonsense. Out of all my years on
the bench, I've never heard of such
a thing.

(Puts on his glasses and picks up a
documented letter form and scans
over it with his eyes, and up at Robert.)

Oh, yes, here it is. If the female
defendant was, uh, uh, er.

ROBERT M. MORRIS
(Turns and smiles at the jurors, interrupts.)

Pregnant, Your Honor, sir, with her
child. But if the court prefers, "flesh," yes.

JUDGE HARDY
(Frowns)

Okay, okay, counselor, if the
"Negro defendant" was pregnant
with this so called, fetus, at
what stage was the Negro called
suppose to be living in.

ROBERT M. MORRIS
(Walks over and stands in front of the Judge.)

Your Honor, sir, Mrs. Sadie Harris
was in her fifth month of pregnancy
when she and her husband,
Frederick, were attacked at Henry
Pop Myers gas station, Sunday
evening, August fourth, nineteen
fifty-six, by two deputies from
Running Creek County Sheriff's
department.

The courtroom becomes silent as Judge Hardy continues to read from the material in front of him. Robert M. Morris watches the Judge patiently. He scans his eyes around the courtroom at the jurors one by one, and at the pictures hanging on the walls around the courtroom of the past great men in their confederate uniforms of the past wars. At the neatly pressed confederate flag displayed on the wall in back of the Judge's seat neatly pressed and clean. Robert slowly looks back over at the Judge who's smiling back at him and said:

JUDGE HARDY
(Holding up a letter in his left hand.)

Okay, counselor, let's just say if
the "Negro' female defendant,"
was really pregnant with a Negro
baby. According to this letter I
have up here in my hand from the
doctor's report, the Negro baby
probably would have inevitably died
anyway because of breathing
problem, true?

ROBERT M. MORRIS
(Walks over in front of the jurors.)

That's true, ladies and gentlemen
of the jury. Any fetus born at
this stage, such as the
defendant's, Mrs. Sadie Harris,
five months into her pregnancy when
she and her husband, Frederick,
were arrested at the crime scene,
might have inevitably died.

JUDGE HARDY
(Smiles.)

Then, Mr. Morris, how can you stand
there and try to bring murder
charges to the county sheriff's
department of Running Creek County,
Alabama, when the Negro child would
have probably died anyway.

ROBERT M. MORRIS
(Turns towards the jurors and speaks back to
the Judge without looking at him.)

Well, Your Honor, I think only you
can answer that for me and the
jurors if you just read a little
further down, sir.

(Smiles at the jurors.)

The courtroom becomes silent. Everyone watches the Judge as he scans over the letter word for word. His eyes are rotating up and down, side to side, determine to find what possibly Robert Mr. Morris is trying to prove to the jury. Finally, the Judge's eyes stop reading suddenly, and he mumbles to himself out loud to the court. He looks over at the prosecutor, who stares b ack at the Judge. He slowly looks over at Robert M. Morris standing next to the jury box.

ROBERT M. MORRIS

Well, Your Honor, can you tell the
jury and myself please, how the
Harris couple and I might be able
to bring felony charges against the
County of Running Creek Alabama.

JUDGE HARDY
(Quickly looks over at the jurors holding the letter in his hand.)

Well, ladies and gentlemen of the
jury, according to this doctor's
report in my hand, it said,
"there's only a chance that the
fetus would have died"

ROBERT M. MORRIS
(Quickly walks over in front of the Judge and spins around to the
Jury, interrupts.)

Absolutely, ladies and gentlemen of
the jury, only a chance that the
Harris child would have lived too,
if the defendants, Sadie and
Frederick, had a chance to get to
the hospital before they were
falsely arrested for a crime they
didn't commit. Henceforth, the
Harris child also could have been
kept alive in an incubator too,
until the child was strong enough
to breath on its own!

END OF SCENE

CHAPTER 9

THE JURY CONSISTED OF SEVEN MEN AND FIVE WOMEN. THE FOREMAN, BEING A GOOD DEAL YOUNGER THAN MOST OF THE OTHER JURORS, HESITATES TO PLAY THE ROLE OF A STRONG CHAIRMAN, AND THE DISCUSSION, UNDISCIPLINED, LEAPS FROM TOPIC TO TOPIC WITH DISCUSSIONS AND CROSS-TALK SLICING THROUGH THE MAIN DELIBERATION.

Bobby Mullen- 20's old Irish minister, seven feet tall with auburn hair. Just the sight of this tall man, large hands, big feet, is very intimidating to the other jurors. Bobby never raises his voice during the deliberation. He just sits and smiles ate everyone around him and quotes from his Bible.

BOBBY MULLEN

Okay members of the jury, there are two ways I think we should look at this case, but, God only knows the truth. However, one, the deputies said the Negroes were caught at the murder scene. And two, the Negroes claim they were on their way to the hospital to have their baby delivered. Now, the question is everyone, who are you going to believe my brothers or sisters?

Bill Dougherty is a 52-year-old
Irish man. He's wearing a dirty,
greasy looking baseball cap. His
dirty white sneakers and shoe
lances are untied. His clothes are
an extra size to large, and his
hands are washed but, his
fingernails still show the dirt
embedded under them from the years
working as an automobile mechanic.

BILL DOUGHERTY
(Smiles at Bobby Mullen, some of his front teeth are missing.)

Yes sir, minister, who is telling
the truth, right?

BOBBY MULLEN
(Smiles at Bill Dougherty.)

Yes, my brother, exactly. That's
why we were chosen out of many to
decide the defendant's fate.

SALLY DIMARTINO IS A SHORT, PRETTY ITALIAN GIRL,
WITH WIDE HIPS AND A SHAPELY FIRM BODY TO
MATCH. SHE'S EARLY 30'S SHE'S 31 YEARS OLD.

SALLY DIMARTINO
(Smiles, scratches her rose tattoo.)

Personally, Mr. Mullen, I don't
believe what those two deputies
said. A lot of things they said
didn't make much sense to me.

(She looks over at Nicky and winks her eye at him, slowly
Rubbing her pencil up and down between her cleavage.)

NICKY BRUNO IS AN ITALIAN MAN, SIX FEET TALL,
FORTY YEARS OLD, WEIGHS OVERT TWO HUNDRED
POUNDS. HE NEVER SPEAKS UNLESS SPOKEN TO. HE HAS
A VERY COOL DEMEANOR. NICKY IS ALWAYS SMILING
AT EVERYONE. ESPECIALLY THE WOMEN OF THE JURY.
HE HAS A HABIT OF UNDRESSING THE FEMALE JURORS
WITH HIS GRAY COLORED EYES.

NICKY BRUNO
(Counting his money under the table as he speaks.)

Yeah, Mullen, that's the way the
colored attorney makes it sound
too. It sounds to me like a
perfect case of false arrest, a
frame-up, lies, and all other kinds
of shit.

(He looks up at Sally's breast, and at Mullen.)

But then again, Mullen, the
deputies probably didn't know what
to think if what the colored
attorney say is true. What I mean
is, look, the deputies walk into
Henry Pop Myers' gas station, see a
colored man standing over a dead
body on the floor in a pool of
blood, just what the hell do you
think the deputies were supposed to
do?

SABRINA CAPALETTI IS ANOTHER SHORT ITALIAN GIRL WITH SHORT DARK BROWN HAIR. LARGE BREASTED EARLY 30'S

SABRINA CAPALETTI

That's right, everybody, what were the deputies supposed to do? I mean, listen, if you were in the deputies' shoes and walk into a murder scene and see the suspect standing there in the victim's blood, what would you have done? I agree with Nicky, they had to do what they had to do to apprehend the criminals.

JENNY WIENSTOCK IS A JEWISH OLD- FASHION FARM GIRL. EARLY 40'S

JENNY WIENSTOCK

No, Sabrina, I don't think that gives the deputies the right to beat the defendants that way even if they are guilty or not. What if the defendants were your children at that station? Would you agree then, that the deputies had the authority to beat the shit out of your kids?

EVA STILLMAN IS A 70-YEAR-OLD SPUNKY GERMAN FEMALE WHO LOOKS YOUNGER THAN SHE REALLY IS.

EVA STILLMAN

Look, everyone, in my opinion, the
colored defendants don't look like
murderers to me. I don't think
they would hurt a fly. If they
needed money that bad, they
probably would be living over by
the graveyard with them other
colored people. Not up here near
us. Don't you agree?

NICKY BRUNO

No, Mrs. Stillman, it doesn't
matter where you live or who you
are, if you have that criminal
element of the mind, you'd go to
any extreme to get your message
across. That too, Mrs. Stillman,
includes the defendant's wife. She
should go down with her husband
because she was the lookout for
him. She's just as much involves in
the murder!

HARRY COHEN IS A JEWISH MAN, A 40 YEARS OLD, AND
WEIGHS OVER 250 POUNDS.

HARRY COHEN
(Sitting in a chair with this head against the wall, eyes
bloodshot, his head bobbing, he looks up and stutters.)

That's right, Nicky, lock her up.
She's in on it too.
(He doses back a sleep.)

SUSAN GOLDBERG MID-30'S YEAR OLD JEWISH WOMAN
WHO ALWAYS LOOKS SLEEPY. SHE IS TALL AND SKINNY
WITH SHORT BLONDE HAIR.

SUSAN GOLDBERG

No, no, no, Harry and Nicky, are
you really going to tell us that
you're willing to convict the
female colored defendant of murder
just because she walked into the
station?

EVA STILLMAN

Well, has anyone ever thought, if
the defendants really murdered
Henry, why didn't they run when
they had the chance to? I can't
believe the colored boy would have
stood there after shooting someone.

Why would his wife walk in
afterwards, if she was supposed to
be out in the car?

JENNY WEINSTOCK

But wait a minute everyone, listen
to yourselves. The Deputies story
differed on a lot of important
things. Don't forget, if the
colored defendant supposed to have
shot Henry Pop Myers in the back,
and the Deputies caught his
standing with the victim's blood

all over him, how in the hell did
he gets the blood all over him in
the first place?

BILL DOUGHERTY

Quite naturally, Jenny. If someone
was to get shot in the back, the
force of the bullet will throw you
forward. Why would anyone want to
shoot Henry for anyway? All anyone
had to do was push him, and he
probably fall on his ass.

BOBBY MULLEN

That doesn't make sense, mu
brothers and sisters. It doesn't
matter what type of gun was used.
the gun doesn't kill people. The
person pulling the trigger does the
killing.

(Opens bible and reads.)

And we all must remember like in
the Bible, Roman's 1:32, and
Roman's 2:1-2, "Who, knowing the
judgment of God, that they which
commit such things are worthy of
death, not only do the same, but
have pleasure in them that do them.
Therefore, thou art inexcusable, O
man, whosoever thou art that
judges: for wherein thou judge
another, thou condemn thyself;

for thou that judges do the same
things. But we are sure that the
judgement of God is according to the
truth against them which commit
such things."

HARRY COHEN
(Sitting in his chair with his back up against the wall, slowly looks
up, bloodshot eyes, head bobbing, stuttering.)

Amen, Brother Mullen, amen.
(He falls back asleep.)

EVA STILLMAN

You know what's bothering me about
this whole shooting business
everyone. If the colored boy
suppose to have shot Henry in the
back several times, and Henry's
dead body had falling forward away
from the colored boy, that means
the colored boy should have been
caught standing at Henry's feet?

BILL DOUGHTERY
As he speaks the jurors nearby hold up
their hands to protect themselves
from his spiting.

You know everybody, the defendant
could have moved around the dead
body after shooting Henry Pop Myers
in the back.

RICHARD THOMPSON IS A GERMAN MAN. 40 YEARS OLD, AND A HOMOSEXUAL.

RICHARD THOMPSON

Excuse me, Mr. Dougherty, before
you spit, ah, ah, I mean speak.
That doesn't make much sense to me.
If I had just shot someone, I would
have been running my sweet ass the
hell, out of there. What the hell
would the defendant be walking
around the dead body for!
After the drawn-out discussion,
Bobby Mullen scribbles a note to
Justice John Hady, and everyone
goes back into the courtroom again.

James O'Connor and Robert M. Morris are fairly calm, feeling it unlikely that the jury had reached a verdict in only a little over an hour. The defendants, Sadie and Frederick Harris, however, are pale and sick with fear.

The suspense is over in a moment. Justice John hardy announces that it is time to go to lunch. During the lunch recess the court reporter locates the various parts of the transcript that the jury wants to reread. He reads out loud the foreman's note naming the sections and discusses it with the jury. Robert M. Morris could tell he was in for a long, tedious afternoon and an even longer wait for the verdict. After lunch everyone sits and listens to the court reporter drone on until late afternoon. Then the jury returns to it's room, the defendants are sent back to their holding cell, and the lawyers resume their efforts to pass the time.

It was disappointing to discover that the rereading had resolved only minor issues. But, although the details of the discrepancy as to the evidence are not very clear in everyone's mind, clarity is no guide to deciding what is true and what is false. Also clear were the many trifling differences among the confessions and evidence, but it is not at all certain that these differences are reason enough to doubt the confessions or to suppose they are guilty or innocent in the eyes of the jury.

Several of the older and more conservative jurors finally express impatience with the discussion, one of them summing up her viewpoint succinctly:

EVA STILLMAN

Look, everybody, I really didn't
think jury duty was gonna take all
day.

(My cats haven't been fed, and I know
they're wondering what the
hell happen to me!)

BOBBY MULLEN

Well, either you believe what the
Deputies said, or you don't. If
you do, admitting, of course, that
deputies can make errors of
judgment, then the questions and
answers were all the evidence
needed to convict the defendants.
The time discrepancy was not the
defendant's fault. It was the
result of being at the wrong place
at the wrong time.

Shortly after 5:00 PM the deliberations are interrupted by the court-room officer who asks he jurors to follow him back into the court-room, bringing their belongings.

There, Justice Hardy tells them they would now be taken out to din-ner, and they were not to discuss the case until they got back. They enjoyed a pleased Italian restaurant, but dinner is a chore. No wine or cocktails permitted, and since the one topic in which they had a common interest was banned, they can only talk self-consciously and dispiritedly about neutral subjects, It was a relief to return to the jury room at 8:00 PM.

All evening long, the plaintiff lawyer, James O'Connor, and the defense lawyer, Robert M. Morris, the clerk of the court and the courtroom attendants keep their dreary vigil, some trying to work, other reading newspapers and magazine, some making sporadic con-versation. The lawyers hope this part of the trial will be over merci-fully soon, but know better. It is common knowledge that the longer a case lasts, the longer it generally takes the jury to arrive at its verdict.

The courtroom becomes a cheerless place, drab and bleakly lit, tomb-like and resounding to every moment. Robert M. Morris, exuding confidence, becomes annoyed at the waste of his evening, and keeps making trips to the phone booth in the lobby.

Downstairs in the holding cell, Frederick and Sadie Harris are endur-ing the same torment they have become accustom to.

Frederick becomes very restless and begins to pace back and forth. Sadie sits in the corner and stares in a daze. She's jumpy and tense. Every once in a while, she sings and rocks slowly back and forth.

Robert M. Morris presumption of Frederick and Sadie's guilt, a phrase he had heard a hundred times, has no real meaning to him anymore, and he does not for an instant expect the jurors to presume them innocent. But Robert decided that he'll fight the case regardless just to find an edge.

The evening wore on with infinite slowness as the jurors struggle back and forth over the muddy, trampled ground of their deliberation. The discussion went on and on, unresolved. Six said not guilty, the other six guilty. The mood of a couple more jurors has swung the other way as the case against the defendants had come to seem more clear-cut, than they had first thought. Still, the discussion went on and on, unresolved, the air grew heavy. Some of them looked at their watches and shook their heads doleful, realizing that they would not get home until very late, or might even have to stay in a hotel overnight and continue in the morning.

The latter proved to be the case. At 10:00 PM, Justice John Hardy, placid and weary eyed, summoned everyone back to the courtroom and announced a recess for the night.

A court van took the jurors to a motel a couple of miles away from the courthouse, stopping en-route at a store that was opened all night to let the them buy toothbrushes, soap razors, and mouth wash. In the morning, angry and seedy in their stale clothing, they breakfasted in a dinner and arrived back at the courthouse by 8:00AM. It was a crisp, sunny morning, the gray clouds finally had gone, the sky at it's purest blue and the air tangy but soft. Reluctantly the jurors marched inside the courtroom, one by one, and took their seats on a long bench.

As soon as he jurors started talking, they agreed that the first order of business was to ask for the rereading of the confession that Frederick Harris had made to the District Attorney, Prosecutor, Mr. James O'Connor. This might resolve the lingering doubts of any juror who might have changed his or her mind.

FINALLY, THE JURORS ARE USHERED INTO THE COURTROOM WHERE THE JUDGE AND THE LAWYERS,

IN FRESH CLOTHES BUT TIRED-LOOKING, WERE WAITING. FREDERICK AND SADIE HARRIS FATIGUED AND WORRIED LOOKING, STARED AT EVERYONE WITH UNBLINKING EYES.

Justice John Hardy announced the order of business, and there was a faint sigh from Robert M. Morris who had desperately wanted an answer to why his clients were being charged for a murder he knew the defendants couldn't have committed, and yet been afraid to hear it. Because Robert knew, and hoped it wasn't guilty.

Everyone settled back while the court reporter thumbed through his pile of transcripts and began reading to the jurors. On and on he read, sometimes stopping to hunt for the next page, or being interrupted by brief discussions between the lawyers and the Judge.

The jurors listened, and stared at the walls or looked unseeing at the secondhand rotating around the clock on the wall, or glances out the window at nothing but blue sky. It went on all morning.

Not until a little before noon did the court reporter stop and announced,

"That's the end of it."

(There's a moment of silence.)

BOBBY MULLEN

"May we go, Your Honor?"

"Yes,"

JUSTICE JOHN HARDY,

"they could."

The jurors returned to their room, ordered sandwiches and soda, and fell to work discussing what they had just heard.

> Doggedly, but with a sense of
> impending defeat, the jurors
> tackled the murder case of the
> defendants once again. No new
> arguments were made, no new
> suggestions were offered; the six
> for conviction were unshakable, but
> the six for acquittal, no longer a
> defensive minority, were self-
> confident and unyielding.

> Beverly Taylor, who had been the
> last to switch to innocent became
> outspoken, after being quiet
> through much of the proceeding.

JUSTICE JOHN HARDY SET A DATE TO HEAR JAMES O'CONNOR ARGUE THAT THE DEADLOCKED VERDICT AGAINST THE DEFENDANTS WAS INCONSIDERATE, AND HE MOTIONED FOR A NEW DAY AND TIME FOR THE NEXT TRIAL. THE JURORS WERE ASKED ONE BY ONE TO AFFIRM THAT THEY FOUND THE DEFENDANTS CASE DEADLOCKED. FINALLY, JUSTICE JOHN HARDY THANKED THAT JURORS FOR THEIR ANTICIPATION DURING THE TRIAL, AND FOR RENDERING A VERDICT ACCOURDING TO THEIR BELIEFS. WITH THAT, THE TRIAL WAS OVER, AND THE JURORS GOT UP, MARCHED OUT OF THE JURY BOX AND WALKED AWAY.

It was 4:00 PM, the courtroom was empty and Justice John Hardy was in his chambers signing the last of papers and preparing to go home. There's a knock on the door, and James O'Connor, weary-eyed, walks in quickly up to the Judge's desk and said:

JAMES O'CONNOR

I just can't understand the jury's
verdict, John. I though the Jury
was working in our favor. But a
deadlock, I couldn't believe my
ears

JUDGE JOHN HARDY
(Sighs, nodding his head.)

I couldn't understand it either,
O'Connor. Now, what in the hell
are we going to do? I was almost
certain the jury were going to
convict those "niggers!"

JAMES O'CONNOR
(Walks back and forth across the room.)

Well, John, I thought we had an air
tight case too, however, some of
the jurors must have looked at the
evidence differently

JUDGE JOHN HARDY
(Follows O'Connor with his eyes as the
prosecutor walks back and forth
slowly across the room in front of his desk,
suddenly smiles, and shouts.)

Yes O'Connor, the Negroes case is
only deadlocked, and it's not
decided yet! We still have another
opportunity, O'Connor, to put those
Negroes in jail.

JAMES O'CONNOR
(Stops directly in front of the
judge's desk as he passes, leans
forward, interrupts.)

No, Your Honor, sir, I'm sorry, I
think the Negroes' case should be
handled by another prosecutor. You
know, sir, maybe we missed
something, and the case can start
fresh again.

(Walks slowly across the room.)

I, I, er, I can't go through
another trial of this sort, Your
Honor, sir.

JUDGE JOHN HARDY
(Quickly stands and leans forward
across his desk and shouts.)

What the hell are you talking
about, O'Connor! No, you can't
give up on me now. You wanted to
take on this case, and I tried to
tell you the best way from the
start how to try these Niggers in
Running Creek County committing
crimes around here! We should have
gotten rid of their bodies when the
deputies had the chance to.

JAMES O'CONNOR

(Quickly stops in front of the
Judge's desk as he walks by, spins
around towards the judge.)

But, but, Your Honor, sir, we can't
keep on doing things this way! You
and I both know the Negro
defendants are innocent. And
hanging innocent people is not the
only way to handle deadlocked
verdicts.

JUDGE HARDY
(Suddenly flops back down into his chair
and contemplates the situation
a moment, drumming his fingers on top of his desk. Pats his foot
quickly against the floor.)

Then how in the hell did you let
that colored attorney beat us,
O'Connor! How will we be able to
face our neighbors, and think of
the embarrassment we would face
from the news media.

JAMES O'CONNOR
(Stares at the Judge a moment, sighs heavy, and slowly walks away a
few feet, and returns and stands in front of the desk.)

Look, Your Honor, sir, I really
don't know what went on inside of
that jury rooms. As I said before,
I thought the case was in our
favor, but, that "colored

attorney" must have proven his
theory to some of the jurors.

JUDGE HARDY
(Quickly stands from his
seat and angrily shouts.)

Then why, O'Connor, after all I've
done for you, you failed! Not only
that, O'Connor, you failed the bar
examination, and it was the
Honorable, Justice John Hardy, who
pulled the strings so you could get
your "'so-called,' law degree,"
remember, it was I, O'Connor! And
you let some, "'colored
crusader," brainwash the jurors
to believe the Negro defendants
were innocent!

(Pointing a gavel at O'Connor as he speaks.)

Now, O'Connor, I know a lot of
people in high places who owe me
favors, and if you know better,
"son," you better not fail me
twice!

JAMES O'CONNOR
(Leans forward against the Judge's desk placing his hands on
top of it as he speaks. Thinks himself a moment, and
stares up at the judge, smiles.)

Your right, sir. No, the case is
not over yet! As you said before,
sir, it's only deadlocked. We have

another golden opportunity to win
this case. Look, Your Honor, I'm
going to file an appeal first thing
in the morning, and we'll see what
happens from there.

AND RELIABLE IT WAS, JAMES O'CONNOR WAS ABLE TO
GET A SECOND TRAIL. O'CONNOR KNEW, WITH ALL
THE CONTRIVANCE THAT TOOK PLACE WITHIN THE
CASE.

The court of Appeals, customarily hears cases for about two weeks
at a time, and then for the next three weeks make their decisions, he
knew another murder would catch their attention.

Furthermore, a fetus, he knew they would want to hear more about
it. After all, the Supreme Court would surely recognize the truth of
the plaintiff, and the defense's argument, and would certainly look
at the trail record and see everything that was wrong. The Supreme
Court, however, was Supreme, and infallible.

Reliable as it was, Robert Morris was able to get a second chance to
prove his theory. First, Robert construed on abortions.

ROBERT MORRIS:

Gentlemen of the jury, ah, er,
abortion is an ancient practice.
It's first performance will never
be known. It is practice by non
literate societies the world over.
The earliest records, Your Honor,
extant, concern themselves with
abortion.

JUDGE ONE
(Smiling)

Well, Mr. Morris, what's your
purpose about abortions?
Ah, just what are your reasons sir?

ROBERT MORRIS

Well, Your Honor, I'm explaining
abortions, or mentioning it,
because I'm trying to show the
court the difference between a
fetus and a human being.
Basically, Your Honor, an infant
child and a fetus.

JUDGE ONE
(Stare questionably)

Well, ah, proceed counselor.

ROBERT MORRIS

Well, Your Honor, the folk
medicine techniques of producing
abortions are legion. One of the
oldest, recommended nearly five
thousand years ago, in Chinese
herbal, involved the use of
mercury, a strong poison. There
were also suggestions involving
physical efforts too.

JUDGE TWO

Physical efforts, counselor, are
you referring to violence?

ROBERT MORRIS

No, Your Honor, sir, such as
climbing a smooth tree or diving
belly flop into the sea from a high
cliff. (Pause and stare)

JUDGE TWO

Hmmm, go on, Mr. Morris.

ROBERT MORRIS

Another prescription was the
application of hot ashes to the
belly or the rubbing of roasted
black beetle powder into the
armpits as well as over the
abdomen. Other recommendations to
produce abortion were to apply
leeches to abdomen, or to eat
certain herb, plants, even insects.
Your Honor, thousands of years ago,
one could also resort to magic.

JUDGE SIX

Magic counselor, are you really
serious?

ROBERT MORRIS

Yes, a matter of fact, in one
record of abortion a medicine man
speaks the girl's initials into a
lemon and utters prayers while the
girl is bathed.

JUDGE SIX

Bathed, Mr. Morris, nude too?

ROBERT MORRIS:
(Snicker)

Yes, Your Honor, whenever he
squeezes a drop of lemon juice on
her head, he urges the as yet
unformed child to emerge before its
time.

JUDGE FIVE

And, Mr. Morris, that's supposed to
be magic?

ROBERT MORRIS

Well, you must remember Your Honor,
that was thousands of years ago.
but today's estimates on the number
of illegal abortions each year in
the United States may vary from
200,000 to 1,5000,000 with
authorities accepting the figure of
1,000,0000. If you compare this

with the current rate of live
births in our country, 4,500,000,
and you will see that nearly one-
fifth of all pregnancies end in
abortions.

JUDGE FIVE

Well, Mr. Morris, these facts are
startling sir. How do you, sir, or
where did you get your facts?

ROBERT MORRIS

Your Honor, research and studies,
and, studies also show that well
over one-half the abortions in our
nation are by married women.

JUDGE THREE

Married women too, why? I thought
the purpose of marriage was to
raise a family, not to destroy a
God given creation, life!

ROBERT MORRIS

Well, plenty of times a woman might
get pregnant and have an abortion,
and her husband wouldn't know the
difference. Also, Your Honor, one
quarter of all women who have ever
been married had undergone an
induced abortion.

JUDGE ONE

Okay, Mr. Morris, we sympathize
with your knowledge of abortions,
but you still haven't answered my
question. What does abortions have
to so with the murder other than,
Henry Pop Myers, are you referring
to? The records show no other
murder was committed, but that of
the deceased!

ROBERT MORRIS

No, you're wrong sir. I'm
referring to the defendant, Sadie
Harris. She was 5 months pregnant
when the defendants were savagely
attacked by the Running Creek
County Deputies, Mr. Jim Jones and
James Smith. Your Honor, they
murdered her innocent child at the
crime scene.

JUDGE ONE
(Shouts)

Innocent child, counselor, there
were no children at the scene of
the crime. It would have been
stated in the arrest report, sir!

ROBERT MORRIS

But, Your Honor, a baby at 5 months
in development has every right as a

child born at 8 months. They're
both human to the naked eye!

JUDGE FOUR
(Shouts)

This is an outrage, counselor. Let
me see if I heard your correct, a
fetus? You're charging the county
of Running Creek, Lexington
Alabama, on no other motive but, a
ball of cells? A tissue of some
sort!

ROBERT HARRIS

Your Honor, please, hear me out.
During the brutality and false
arrest sir, yes, Mr. Fred and Sadie
Harris.

JUDGE FOUR
(Interrupts)

Mr. Morris, sir, we'll be the judge
on any charges. Let's not make any
false accusations!

ROBERT MORRIS
(Grins)

I'm sorry, Your Honor, bur during
the defendant's arrest, Mrs. Harris
was 5 months pregnant. The
defendants were on their way to the
hospital when they stopped to

purchase gas, and Mr. Harris
stumbled across a murder.

JAMES O'CONNOR
(Leaps up from seat)

Objection, Your Honor, the
defendants were caught in the act!
The evidence proves that they were
at the scene of the crime during
the murder!

JUDGE FOUR
(Slams gavel)

Sustained, proceed Mr. Morris.

ROBERT MORRIS

Before the defendants arrived at
the gas station, Your Honor, Henry
Pop Myers had already been murdered
sir.

JUDGE ONE

But, Mr. Morris, how does your
accusations prove that another
murder was committed also? We have
the arrest report, one murder, and
the jury's verdict was deadlocked?

ROBERT MORRIS

Yes, Your Honor, the jury was
deadlocked, and they couldn't

deliver its verdict. The jury
couldn't prove the defendants were
guilty of the crime!

JUDGE FOUR

The deadlocked verdict only proves
that the jury were undecided, Mr.
Morris, that's why the plaintiff
motioned for an appeal. However,
sir, the prosecutor claims the
deadlock verdict was inadmissible
only.

ROBERT MORRIS
(Glances at O'Connor, smiles.)

Or, Your Honor, maybe the
prosecutor's appeal was motioned
for another reason, like a cover-
up, maybe!

JUDGE SIX
(Slams gavel.)

This is the Supreme Court, Mr.
Morris, anymore outbursts of such,
and we'll hold you in contempt of
court, sir!

ROBERT MORRIS
(Sighs)

I'm sorry, Your Honor, I'll
restrain myself. But, Your Honor,
Henry Pop Myers was already

murdered when the defendants
arrived at the scene. Upon
entering the office, Mr. Harris
tripped over the deceased lying on
the floor. He fell into a pool of
blood, lying there a moment in
shock, curious, and confused. Your
Honor, my clients are being framed
for the murder, in which there was
no other evidence during the trail
that could be directed to the
defendant's sir, other than the fact
that they were caught at the murder
scene!

JUDGE ONE

Cover-up, framed, another murder,
Mr. Morris? I heard you say
something of that nature a few
times sir. How does all your
accusations fit into place
counselor? We are trying to figure
out who else was murdered sir.
Henry Pop Myers is the only murder
victim, that's conclusive, but,
we're interested to know where this
child of the defendants was located
during the arrest?

Robert Morris's strategy started to
unfold, he had the panel of judges
right where he wanted his case to
flow. If he could get their ears
open, this would prove his theory,
that the unborn fetus of Sadie

Harris was a human being at the
time of its death. There were two
murders committed at the gas
station, and the defendants were
involved in one of the murders, but
only as one of the victims. Robert
knew you can't commit a crime if
you're a victim of the crime.
Robert Morris: First of all, Your
Honor, when is a fetus considered
human, at birth or from conception?
The panel of judges looks at Robert
with curiosity.

ROBERT MORRIS
(Pause, stares)

Well, gentlemen, actually the first
stage, the Germinal Stage, some
doctors believe, this period from,
fertilization until the end of the
second week after conception is the
beginning of life. This period
ends when the fertilized ovum, or
technically speaking, gentlemen,
the blastocyst, which is your term
given to, "a hollow ball of cells,"
is present during the second week
after conception, is implanted in
the wall of the uterus.

Now gentlemen, you might say to
yourselves, at this stage the
blastocyst is just a hollow ball of
cells, but, actually, this child
has already embedded itself in the

uterine lining sometime during the
second week after conception. Even
afterwards, gentlemen, implantation
occurs about seven days after
conception too. Thus, the actual
Germinal period is somewhat shorter
than two weeks.

JUDGE ONE

How interesting, Mr. Morris, but
how can you consider this being
life already?

ROBERT MORRIS

That's very good question Your
Honor. Some people believe that
this tiny ball of cells can't be
human just because it doesn't have
the ability to run and cry, or,
have features and emotions because
it can't be seen with the naked
eye. But, Your Honor. It has been
to live, and it does have human
features already.

JUDGE TWO

But, Mr. Morris, it can' be seen
with the naked eye. What evidence
do you have that this thing is a
human being?

ROBERT MORRIS

Because, Your Honor, at this second
stage of life, the Embryonic stage,
the six-week period from the end of
the second week until the end of
the second month after conception,
the first bone cell is laid down.
You may not believe it still,
gentlemen, but this microscopic
cell has human bones too.

JUDGE FOUR
(Interrupts)

One bone cell, Mr. Morris, and
you're trying to convince the
Supreme Court, this thing should be
considered a child?

ROBERT MORRIS

Yes, Your Honor, already human
development has occurred.

JUDGE FIVE

Human development, counselor, how
is it human? Does it look like a
child? Does this thing have arms,
legs? You need all these human
parts to be able to consider
something human!

ROBERT MORRIS

That's true, Your Honor, and might
I add, the embryo does have all the
essential human parts, and looks to
a practiced eye like a tiny human
being.

JUDGE FOUR

A what, Mr. Morris, a tiny human
being?

ROBERT MORRIS

Yes, Your Honor, a tiny human
being! Just because it can't be
seen by the naked eye sir, you
would probably think the embryo
isn't life. And yes, Your Honor,
there are many other professional
people who don't agree either.

JUDGE SIX

Then, Mr. Morris, how can it me
murdered if it can't be seen by the
naked eye?

ROBERT MORRIS

But, gentlemen, you could call it,
what, ah, miniature human being, I
guess-

JUDGE FOUR
(Interrupts)

Wait, Mr. Morris, first, you take
us on a journey from a hollow ball
of cells to a tiny human being, and
now, it's a miniature human being?

ROBERT MORRIS

But first, Your Honor, are you
convinced it's human?

JUDGE FOUR

Look, counselor, we're not doctors,
how do we know.

ROBERT MORRIS

But, Your Honor, sir, no, one has to
be a doctor to know about life if
something grows, breaths, and dies,
it was once considered life.

JUDGE FIVE

Okay counselor, then how do you
know these feet stages are human
too?
This feet stage, where did it get
feet from?

ROBERT MORRIS
(Giggles)

Fetal sir, I said the "fetal
stage."

JUDGE SIX

Well, Mr. Morris, if the defendant
loss her child, what stage is this
fetal stage? How do we know that
this black fetus was human at this
stage?

ROBERT MORRIS

Because Your Honor, the fetal stage
is called the developing baby.
It's the same fetal stage as a
Developing white fetus, sir!

JUDGE FOUR

A what, counselor, a developing
baby?

ROBERT MORRIS

Yes, Your Honor, the developing
child! It's the technical dividing
point between the embryonic and
fetal staged. It's the appearance
of the first real bone cells that
begin to replace the cartilage.

JUDGE ONE
(INTERRUPTS)

Cartilage, Mr. Morris, what stage
is that? How do we know if this
stage is another human stage of
life?

ROBERT MORRIS
(Smiles)

That's a very good question, Your
Honor. From the very second stage,
when I mentioned the first bone
cell laid down, well, sir, this is
another such stage of the child's
life.

JUDGE THREE

Oh, yeah, counselor, the Embryonic
stage, wasn't it?

ROBERT MORRIS
(Smiles)

Yes, sir, and now this fetal stage
of cartilage, is the very same
bones you fine gentlemen are
sitting on, and, the very same
bones I'm standing on today in
court.

JUDGE TWO

Cartilage, Mr. Morris. And you
still want us to decide a verdict
on cartilage sir? What type of
life does this cartilage have to
consider you to make us believe
it's part human?

ROBERT MORRIS

Well, sir, I can only say, this
material of cartilage you're
referring to is the very same
material from which the soft part
of your nose is made from. And if
you squeeze it very hard sir, I'm
sure, you would feel the pain.

JUDGE ONE
(Sighs.)

Well, Mr. Morris, human lecture,
I'm quite sure there's a good
reason for this educational lesson
pertaining to your case sir.

ROBERT MORRIS

Why, yes, Your Honor, there is.

JUDGE TWO

Well, counselor, are you finished
with delivering babies?

ROBERT MORRIS
(Snickers)

Actually sir, I'm not but, I would just like to elaborate on one more thing about the fetus, with your permission.

JUDGE TWO
(Sighs.)

Go on Mr. Morris, what else?

ROBERT MORRIS

Gentlemen, the fetal period lasts seven months and is the longest of the prenatal stages. The main events of this period includes a substantial increase in fetal size along with an elaboration and growth of the bodily structures laid down during the Embryonic stage. And, if you have forgotten, the embryonic stage was the one when the first bone cell was laid down.

JUDGE FOUR

Yes, er, ah, Mr. Morris, didn't you say it couldn't be seen with the naked eye sir?

ROBERT MORRIS
(SMILES.)

That's correct, Your Honor. I also
said you would probably think it
wasn't human either because of that
fact too. But, I also said it was
the initial start of human life.

JUDGE FIVE

Oh yeah, Mr. Morris, I remember
that too.

ROBERT MORRIS

Then, gentlemen, when does human
life begins? Is it the first
initial point of conception, or,
only when the infant is cut from
The umbilical cord of it's mother?
the Supreme Court judges are
stalled for a moment, watching
Robert Morris thinking to
themselves. Some rested their
heads on their hands, some on their
chins, others scratching their
heads, unable to answer until Judge
One decides to take a chance.

JUDGE ONE

Well, Mr. Morris, you've certainly
have done your homework. But what
does all this have to do with the
murder of the victim, ah, er, ah,

it's purpose? We are not here to
discuss prenatal care, or the
medical terminology of the facts of
life sir. We're all here today on
the account of the murder of Henry
Pop Myers, the deadlocked verdict,
in case you've forgotten!

ROBERT MORRIS

Your Honor, sir, I know the purpose
of this argument proceeding and,
ah, er, the jurors couldn't reach
an agreement on whether my clients
were guilty or innocent.

JUDGE TWO

Also, counselor, remember too, that
the deadlock verdict was only a
result of not being able to decide.
some felt they were guilty, the
others didn't. Who's right, and
who's wrong!

ROBERT MORRIS

Yes, Your Honor, I understand.

JUDGE FOUR

No, ah, counselor Morris, I don't
Think you do. An agreement hasn't
been reached, so until we can reach
a final verdict here, they're
guilty just the same!

JAMES O'CONNOR

But, Your Honor, sir, those were my
whole intentions for my motion for
this appeal. We found the
defendants guilty and the jurors
verdict came to a deadlock

JUDGE THREE
(Interrupts.)

Excuse me, Mr. O'Connor, we are
quite aware of this appeal. This
is the Supreme Court, and we'll
have the final say. Until we reach
the final argument, the defendants
are innocent to the court until we
find not, understand sir?

JAMES O'CONNOR

Yes, Your Honor, I understand sir.

JUDGE SIX
(Interrupts.)

Mr. O'Connor, sir, what do you mean
when you said you found the
defendants guilty? I don't believe
any charges have been filed yet.
You said yourself, sir, the jury
was deadlocked!

ROBERT MORRIS
(Looks at O'Connor, smiles.)

Yes, Mr. O'Connor, I would like to
Know too, how the verdict was
deadlocked but, you find the
defendants guilty?

JUDGE FIVE

Mr. Morris, sir, you're out of
order again. We'll be the judge of
that, and we'll ask all the
questions. You are here to argue
your case, you are not here to ask
any questions upon our asking.

ROBERT MORRIS

I'm sorry, Your Honor. I'm just
trying to figure out something, if
the jury came to a deadlock but,
the prosecutor still insists on
convicting the defendants?

JUDGE THREE

Excuse me, Mr. Morris, must I
remind you too, until we reach the
final argument, the defendants are
only innocent until we have the
final say!

JAMES O'CONNOR
(Stands up quickly.)

But, Your Honor, if person with
legal malice commits an act or sets
off chain of events from which,
these are common behaviors among
the Niggas living in Running Creek
county sir, make the defendants
just as wrong as the others?

ROBERT MORRIS
(Stands up quickly.)

Objection, Your Honor, common
events among a person does not
pertain to all people of the same
color! And there are no such
records, or proof, of the
defendants engaging in any other
such malice of the sort!

JUDGE ONE:

Sustained, Mr. Morris!

JAMES O'CONNOR
(Smiles.)

Thank you, Your Honor, but, it is
natural or reasonable foreseeable
results that person or persons are
guilty of murder, if death results
from act, or from events, which it
naturally produced, and, Your
Honor, if original malicious act

was either arson, rape kidnapping,
burglary, or which that the
defendants committed, robbery and
murder in the first degree!

ROBERT MORRIS
(Interrupts.)

Objection, Your Honor, the juror's
verdict was deadlocked, and also,
because of judicial errors they
were apt to have combined elements
from the co-defendant and that of
which, confessions of the Deputies,
Mr. Jimmy Jones and James Smith, of
Running Creek County, in the
reading, the verdict of deadlocked.

JAMES O'CONNOR:
(Stands up quickly.)

Objection!

JUDGE TWO

Sustained, proceed Mr. Morris.

ROBERT MORRIS

Thank you, sir, and Your Honor, the
court errored in admitting the
testimony of the defendants in
relationship to the dying
declaration of Henry Pop Myers.

JAMES O'CONNOR

Objection, Your Honor!

JUDGE TWO

Sustained, proceed Mr. Morris.

ROBERT MORRIS

Your Honor, because the
declarations were not made by the
decease under any apprehension of
death, as expressed directly or
indirectly, by himself.

JAMES O'CONNOR

Objection, Your Honor, the victim
was murdered in cold blood when the
defendants were apprehended at the
scene of the crime.

ROBERT MORRIS
(Quickly stands.)

Because, Your Honor, the
admissibility of dying
declarations, depends upon the
apprehension of the part making
them, and should not have been
inferred by the Justice, John
Hardy, from other testimony in the
defendant's trial. Other evidence,
Very material to the defendants,
has been discovered since the

trail, which I had no previous knowledge of, or opportunity of procuring, and which will show the innocence of the defendants!

JAMES O' CONNOR

Objection, the evidence, Your Honor, the victim's blood on the defendant and the co-defendant's clothes, were caught at the scene of the crime. The defendant's footprints in the mud to and from the office to their car.

JUDGE TWO

Sustained, Mr. O'Connor.

ROBERT MORRIS
(Smiles.)

Thank you, sir. On the other hand, gentlemen, before the defendants can be convicted of murder, the jury must be satisfied, not only that the defendants has committed this felonious homicide with which they're being framed, er, ah, excuse me please, charged with, but that, in it's perpetration, they intended to take away the life of it's victim,

JUDGE ONE

Well, Mr. Morris, what were the
defendant's perpetration's?

ROBERT MORRIS

The defendant's intentions were
only to purchase gasoline, and not
to create any crime!

JAMES O'CONNOR

Objection, Your Honor, no other
Evidence to my knowledge has been
Discovered.

JUDGE ONE

Sustained counselor.

ROBERT MORRIS
(Smiles at O'Connor.)

Ah, gentlemen, with your
permission, I would like to direct
your attention to the Medical
Examiner's report of the State of
Alabama Coroner's office, which has
been laid before your eyes. I
asked, Steve Stillman, the chief
doctor of the coroner's office to
give me the futures on the time of
death of Henry Pop Myers.
The panel of judges pick through
their paper work in front of them

until they discover their copy of
the report. Robert waits until
they all look up at him.

ROBERT MORRIS
(Smiles.)

If you haven't notice, Your Honor,
the time of death according to the
Deputies, Mr. Jones and Smith,
presented before your eyes too, was
recorded at 10:00 AM, when the
defendant's were apprehended at the
murder scene.
The panel of judges pick through
their paper work again, Robert
waits until they look up at him.

ROBERT MORRIS

So, gentlemen, Mr. Stillman's
actual time of death was recorded
somewhere around 9:00 AM, which
Means, according to this theory, if
the defendants were apprehended by
the Deputies at, or around, 10:00
AM, and if you agreed with the
deputies testimony, then, the
defendants are, without a doubt,
guilty. They were caught in the
act of murdering Henry Pop Myers.
Robert Morris stalls, and waits a
moment until this theory sinks into
the minds of the judges.

ROBERT MORRIS

> Or, gentlemen, if you agreed with
> Doctor Stillman's recorded time of
> death, at, or around 9:00 AM, and
> still disbelieve Sadie and
> Frederick Harris are innocent,
> which can only mean one thing, the
> murder mush have been committed an
> hour earlier upon the defendants
> stumbling across this gruesome
> scene!

The courtroom becomes still and quiet. Robert Morris slowly turns and stares at everyone. The judges and the prosecutor appears to be in their own thoughts. The Public Defender's accusations were the only logical ones that of the prosecutor's. But the panel of judges put up a last minute fight to conclude the conceivable results.

JUDGE ONE
(Rubbing eyes, sighs, and stares at O'Connor.)

> Okay, Mr. O'Connor, according to
> the deputies time of death, or
> discovery of the body, there seems
> to be an hour difference sir.

James O'Connor appears to be sweating, nervous, he wipes his forehead with a handkerchief he takes out of his pocket. Both judges begin to move silently towards each other whispering. Finally, Judge Six put up a last-minute fight to conclude his thoughts.

JUDGE SIX
(Grins.)

Mr. O'Connor, sir, if you could
answer one question, a simple yes
Or no would do, I think you could
solve this whole case all by
yourself. Ah, tell us, Mr.
O'Connor, was the deputies
discovery of the deceased correct
or not?

JAMES O'CONNOR
(Pause, stares at the panel of judges, his voice muffled.)

Yes, Your Honor.

The panel of judges unable to hear clearly O'Connor's answer, turns
and glances at one another slowly back and forth until Judge One
puts up another last-minute fight to conclude the conceivable results.

JUDGE ONE
(Moments past, stares at Robert Morris who is daydreaming.)

Mr. Morris, sir, are there anymore
questions? Why are you sitting
there like a deaf-mute?

ROBERT MORRIS
(Snaps out of his thought.)

Er, er, ah, Your Honor, sir, were
you speaking to me?

JUDGE ONE

Yes, counselor, I was. I said, are
there anymore charges or arguments
for the court to hear? However,
sir, you had mentioned something
about another murder committed.
I'm still confused about something
sir, had a child been murdered too,
the trial records would have said
so, Henry Pop Myers is the only
victim.

ROBERT MORRIS

Yes, Your Honor, I would like to
motion for an Amendment. Another
murder was committed during that of
Henry Pop Myers. The defendants
were victims of cruel inhuman
punishment. All the reasons
presented for a new trial were laid
before your eyes gentlemen. My
reasons are for the merits of this
case, the defendants are
charging the County of Running
Creek, Lexington, Alabama, with
murder in the first degree for
their child!

JUDGE TWO
(Sighs)

But Mr. Morris, sir, the only way
for your Amendment are on the
grounds of circumstantial evidence.

ROBERT MORRIS

Yes, Your Honor, I would say it's
somewhat circumstantial. The
defendant's fetus was life before
it was murdered in cold blood too!

JUDGE TWO

Of course, Mr. Morris, that it
could not have been obtained at the
former trail with reasonable
diligence used by the defendants.

ROBERT MORRIS

Yes, Your Honor, I understand.

JUDGE SIX

And, Mr. Morris, your testimony
must be merely cumulative and
corroborative of other testimonies
given in the case. It must not be
merely for the purpose of
impeaching the credibility of
witnesses and it must be such as if
must prove or produce a different
Verdict. These are the reasons for
any purpose for your new trail, any
new trial before they're granted,
Mr. Morris, are you ready?

ROBERT MORRIS

Yes, Your Honor, I'm aware of this.

JUDGE SIX
(Smiles at the other judges.)

On what grounds are you seeking an
amendment, Mr. Morris?

ROBERT MORRIS

The defendants are charging murder
against the deputies of Running
Creek County, Lexington Alabama,
Mr. Jimmy Jones and James Smith, on
or about 10:00 AM, at Henry Pop
Myers gas station out on the new
highway extension of route 69.
James O'Connor, reading over the
Public Defender's Amendment would
change the course of the trial,
decides his defeat and starts
putting his records and belongings
into his briefcase. Afterwards,
rises from the table to exit.

JUDGE FIVE
(Looks up.)

Ah, Mr. O'Connor, sir, ah, courts
still in session.

JAMES O'CONNOR
(Giggles.)

Oh, ah, Your Honor, I was just
going to the bathroom.

JUDGE FOUR

Yes, we see that sir, but do you
always go to the bathroom with your
briefcase?

JAMES O'CONNOR
(Snickers.)

Oh, my Briefcase, this,
(He lays it back on the table.)

Ah, you know how it is, Your Honor,
you carry those things so much,
it's hard to let go.

James O'Connor enters the bathroom and looks up at the window. The window is half opened, and a small bird flutters on the sill, then fly away. He sits on the toilet stool with his pants on. He thinks about Judge Hardy's arbitrary scheme to protect the fate of the count's reputation and his nephew, and what a fool he's been. He begins to visualize Judge Hardy ridiculing him in his chambers. He visualizes himself handcuffed, standing in front of a black judge, whose pointing his gavel at him. Moments past, O'Connor snaps back into reality when he hears a knock and a voice at the door. "Mr. O'Connor, we're ready to proceed sir.

JAMES O'CONNOR
(Rushes back to his seat, sitting down.)

I'm sorry, Your Honor, I was just
thinking about something.

ROBERT MORRIS
(Interrupts, leans towards O'Connor.)

You could have escaped through the
window, O'Connor, no bars.

JAMES O'CONNOR
(Quickly turns away from Robert towards the Judges.)

I'm sorry, Your Honor, sir, I'm
ready to proceed.

JUDGE ONE
(Sighs, rubs forehead.)

Okay gentlemen, we've heard enough
at this point. As matter of
fact, it's sort of puzzling. A
murder has been committed,
according to the State Coroner's
Office one-hour difference from
that of the deputy's discovery an
hour later, but, the Public
Defender claims another murder has
occurred too.
But, there were no other murdered
victims found at the scene.

JAMES O'CONNOR
(Interrupts.)

And, Your Honor, the footprints
were made by the defendants, to and
from their car they used during the
crime.

ROBERT MORRIS

Objection, Your Honor! If this is
true, how could, or, why would the
defendant's run back and forth
repeatedly?

JAMES O'CONNOR
(STANDS QUICKLY.)

Objection, Your Honor, the colored
defendant's were caught at the
crime scene, and Mr. Harris was
standing over the deceased holding
the murder weapon, and, Your Honor,
they both had the victim's blood
all over them! Apparently, the
defendants had to struggle with
Henry Pop Myers.

ROBERT MORRIS
(INTERRUPTS, STANDS QUICKLY.)

Objection, Your Honor, from the
records sir, according to the time
of death of Henry Pop Myers, the
murder had to be committed before
the defendants arrived!

JUDGE SIX
(Tapping gavel, looks at O'Connor.)

But, Mr. O'Connor, there were quite
a number of footprints at the gas
station that day, sir. Whether
they were there an hour earlier of

ROBERT MORRIS

(Quickly shuts his hand and walks back
and forth across the floor in front
of the judges.)

Exactly, Your Honor, what
difference would it make! Plants
of flowers, flowers or plants, what
difference does it make?

(Opens hand exposing the seeds.)

I never said what type of seeds
here in my hand were but, if I
asked you again, were they flowers
or plants in my hand, how would you
respond.

JUDGE FIVE
(Interrupts, quickly sits back in chair.)

Ridiculous, Mr. Morris, how could
those little things in your hand be
flowers or plants, sir, they're
seeds?

ROBERT MORRIS

That's correct, Your Honor,

(points at seeds in hand.)

These little seeds in my hand are
nor flowers or plants yet, until
they are planted, watered, and

sprouts out of the earth, but,
gentlemen, why couldn't they very
well be classified as a flower or a
plant before they're buried and
bloomed.

JUDGE THREE
(Quickly sits back in chair.)

That's impossible, Mr. Morris, how
can those flower or plant seeds be
classified as anything until they
bloom? Until then, counselor,
they're just seeds.

ROBERT MORRIS
(Quickly shuts hand exposing seeds, walks back across the floor.)

But, gentlemen, with the right
nurturing and proper care, these
seeds will grow into a bunch of
flowers or plants.

JUDGE THREE

Look, Mr. Morris, we are not here
to discuss plant life. This is a
murder trial, and we're getting off
track here.

JUDGE FOUR
(Interrupts, sits back in chair.)

Yes, we are, first counselor, you
spoke about the stages of a colored
fetus, and now, sir, you're trying

to convince us that a flower or
plant, what difference it makes,
I'll never know, should have the
same jurisdiction as a fetus? You
know, Mr. Morris, if this has
anything to do with the other
murder you claim was at the scene,
I would like to hear about it?

ROBERT MORRIS
(Nods head yes.)

Well, yes, Your Honor, it does.

JAMES O'CONNOR
(Snickers.)

Excuse me, Your Honor, maybe Mr,
Morris is talking about a pregnant
gardener.

JUDGE SIX
(Interrupts, smiles at O'Connor, frowns at Robert.)

I don't know what to call it but,
Mr. Morris, I keep hearing about
this murdered, or missing colored
child throughout this trial. This,
wouldn't happen to be the same
murder you are referring to, is it?

ROBERT MORRIS
(Spins around at judge.)

Yes, Your Honor, sir, the very same
murdered, or, missing child the co-

defendant, Mrs. Sadie Harris, was
carrying with her to the hospital.

JUDGE FOUR
(Interrupts, picks up report off
The table in front of him, looks at
It as he speaks.)

I don't understand any of this, Mr.
Morris, you keep on insisting a
child was present but, I still
can't find any such statement
clarifying anything of a child
being involved.

ROBERT MORRIS
(Interrupts.)

But, Your Honor, a child was
present. Mrs. Sadie Harris was
pregnant during their arrest. Her
child was ready to be born, on it's
way through the birth canal.

JUDGE FIVE
(Interrupts.)

What now, Mr. Morris, do we have a
doctor in the house? Counselor,
this is a murder trial, and you are
a lawyer, you've studied law. What
gives you the right to know when it
was a child.

JUDGE FOUR
(Interrupts)

And by the way, Mr. Morris, a fetus
it was, and now some child on it's
way through the birth canal.
Furthermore, sir, how can you stand
there and tell the Supreme Court,
the Sheriffs, Department of Running
Creek County should be charge with
murder in the defense of a flower,
er,ah, plant, er, I mean, a fetus?

ROBERT MORRIS

It was child, Your Honor, yes, in
the defense of the child I'm
bringing charges.

JUDGE ONE
Interrupts, looks at his watch, and up at Robert Morris.

Mr. Morris, we're sitting here in
the Supreme Court of Justice, over
the murder of a fetus sir?

ROBERT MORRIS

Apparently, we are, Your Honor, and
the fetus, should have the same
rights of the law as a child you
would have if it ran out into the
road and run over by an eight
Wheeler Mack Truck

JUDGE TWO
(Interrupts.)

But, ah, Mr. Morris, getting back
to the seeds, I'm curious about
your point. What exactly where you
trying to prove?

ROBERT MORRIS

Remember earlier, Your Honor, when
I said a child born at this stage,
which the defendant's child was in.

JUDGE TWO
(Interrupts.)

Yes, the fetus would die, right?

ROBERT MORRIS
(Smiles, points finger at the judge.)

No, I said would inevitably die
since the child was unable to
sustain the necessary breathing
movements.

JUDGE ONE

But the seeds, Mr. Morris, the
seeds sir, what about the seeds?

ROBERT MORRIS
(Opens hand carrying seeds.)

Gentlemen, just like a child, or if
the court prefers, fetus, born at
this early stage of birth will
inevitably die because of breathing
movements, and just like these
seeds in my hand, if I bury them in
the earth, no one really knows if
they will grow. They might bloom,
they might not.

JUDGE TWO
(Interrupts.)

But, how would we know, counselor,
if this child would have lived
anyway?

ROBERT MORRIS
(Opens hand exposing seeds towards Judges.)

Well, gentlemen, just as much of a
chance as these seeds blooming if I
bury them in the earth!

CHAPTER 10

EXT: EVENING: JUDGE'S BEDROOM BARRICADE'S IN BEDROOM

That night before going to sleep, Justice John Hardy, barricades his bedroom door with his dresser and tall bureau. John pours himself a glass of water from his bedroom's night table and washed down a whole bottle of pills and drops the empty bottle on the floor, and gets into bed on his back and closes his eyes.

On the night stand the Judge has left a receipt for the latest payment of his $500,000 life insurance policy, and the names of his insurance agent and attorney, and the benefactor to the Hardy family's legacy.

The Honorable Judge John hardy had purchased the policy after the deadlocked verdict in the Harris trial. However, John also left a note instructing his son, Keith, to pay off all debts, then he and the Judge's young girlfriend, Bunny, and her young daughter, Monica, could use the rest of the money to do as they please.

Later that evening when Keith, Bunny, and Monica return home, Bunny rushes up to the Judge's bedroom. Bunny felt something was wrong when she couldn't open the door completely. She manages to push the door completely open and discovers the Judge lying on his back with the sheets pulled up to his neck. Bunny looks around the Judge's bedroom, and slowly reads the information the Judge had left on his night stand as she picks it up. Bunny smiles as she reads the letter, and glances a few times at the sleeping Judge lying on the bed across from her. Bunny picks up the pillow lying next to the Judge's head, and firmly presses the pillow against the Judge's face and presses down on it very hard until the bed starts rocking up and down a few times.

After a moment, Bunny realizes what she had just done, and steps back away from the bed, and toss the pillow back on top of the Judge's body. Keith, out of breath, suddenly appears at the bedroom door dressed in a dark suit, shirt and tie, startles Bunny. She spins around at Keith, and points, covering her mouth in horror with the other hand, at the Judge and said:

BUNNY
(Speaking while still covering her mouth in horror.)

Oh, Keith, you scared me. I, I, I
think your father is asleep. When
I came up to check on the Judge,
the bedroom furniture was pushed up
against the door like he was trying
to keep us out. I discovered your
father lying just like that on his
back. (Points at the Judge.)

KEITH
(Rushes over to the Judge lying on the bed, picks up his father's wrist and tries to feel for a pulse, and drops his father's hand back to the bed, and spins around at Bunny.)

Look, Bunny, it's okay. Listen,
let me put things back in order. I
want you to go call the Sheriff's
office, and have him send somebody
her quick.

Bunny rushes out of the bedroom and runs downstairs to use the telephone and nervously tries to dial the phone. Meanwhile, Keith rushes back into his bedroom, rummages through his dresser drawer, and suddenly pulls out a hypodermic needle filled with some type of liquid. Keith holds the hypodermic needle up in the air to the light and stares at it a moment, then rushes back into the Judge's bedroom. Keith stops at the side of the Judge's bed, stares At his father a moment, then slowly sits on the side of the bed. Bunny suddenly shouts from down stairs.

BUNNY
(Shouts loudly)

Keith, Keith, the line is busy.
what should we do!

Keith, sitting on the side of the bed, quickly snatches his tie off from around his neck and wraps it tightly around the Judge's dangling arm lying across his lap. He stares at the needle, and then back at his father, and back at the needle.

BUNNY
(Shouts loudly again)

Keith, did you hear me! I said the
line is busy. What are we going to
do now.

KEITH
(Shout's back at Bunny.)

I don't know, damn it, Bunny, just
keep trying until you reach someone.

BUNNY
(Downstairs, holding the mouth piece of the phone, shouts
back upstairs to Keith.)

Oh, Keith, I think I have
somebody on the line now.

Moments pass, Keith's standing up from the bed and smiling back down at his father's dangling arm hanging off the side of the bed with the neck tie still wrapped around its arm, and the hypodermic needle protruding from it.

KEITH
(Standing back away from the bed speaking to the corpse.)

Now, your old crazy bastard, I've
waited so long for the right
opportunity to get rid of your old,
"corrupted ass, father!" You just
couldn't understand I didn't want
to be a lawyer and follow in your
evil shoes. You've treated me like
"shit," because I chose to be a
social worker for Running Creek

County, and tried to bring change
to our community between the
negroes and the white folks.

(Walks back and forth as he speaks.)

So, what did you do, Your Honor
you kept the fuel burning with your
"confederate law of the past."
Against the Negroes of the county,
father, but, Your Honor, sir, never
again, because-

BUNNY
(Downstairs, holding the mouth piece of the phone, shouts.)

Keith, Keith, I have the sheriff on
the line. What should I tell him.

KEITH

Rushes out of the bedroom to the top of the stairs and shouts back down to Bunny.

> Ah, ah,
> (Nervously walks back and forth.)
> I don't know exactly, Bunny, just
> tell the sheriff that my father
> won't answer, or open his bedroom
> door. Ah, I think something's
> wrong. We might need a doctor!

END OF SCENE

CHAPTER 11

EARLY AM- SUNNY DAY- JUDGE HARDY'S RESIDENCE

Early the next day, the morning sun scarcely felt, Keith Hardy was jogging home from his daily three-mile workout, when he stops suddenly and notices the commotion a distance away at his house.

The news reporters and camera crews were asking questions to all the neighbors to see what all the commotion was about.

Two county Deputies were standing at attention outside of Keith's front door, not blinking an eye. The county crime lab technicians were moving swiftly, searching for clues for other probabilities for the cause of death. Suddenly the Outside Deputies step aside, and Deputy Sheriff's, Jimmy Jones and James Smith, were bringing Frederick Harris and

Another house attendant, Pete, handcuffed together, who Keith Hardy had hired both of them after the Harris trial had ended, out into the front yard.

Keith Hardy's eyes stretches with delight seeing his actual plan taking it's course of action. He continues his jogging, out of breath, right up to the arresting deputies and Frederick and Pete, and said:

KEITH HARDY
(Standing in front of Pete, out of breath.)

But, Pete, ah, ah

(he tries to catch his breath.)

Why are they arresting you?

FREDERICK HARRIS
(Steps forward, shouts.)

What the hell is going on, Keith,
why are the deputies arresting me?
I haven't done anything!

PETE
(Shaking his head.)

I haven't done anything either, Mr.
Keith. All I know is, me and
Frederick came to work this
morning, and were in the kitchen
preparing breakfast, and the
deputies came to the house and said
we were being taking down to the
sheriff's office for questioning.
Then, they bring your father out in
a body bag while you were out
jogging. Look, Keith, we had no
idea your father was upstairs dead.
I'm sorry.

FREDERICK HARRIS

I didn't know the Judge was dead
either, Keith. Before I left last
night, I was vacuuming the upstairs
carpet. As I went past the Judges
bedroom, I saw him sitting up in
his bed smiling at me.

KEITH HARDY
(Shaking his head no,)

No, no, no, Frederick! What do you
mean before you left last night?
didn't I instruct you to watch over
the Judge while Miss Bunny and her
daughter and I came back from in
town?

PETE
Smiles, interrupts

But that's all right, Keith, I told
Frederick he could leave. You just
hired him, and he wasn't sure how
to get home from here. I let him
leave while it was still light out
so, Frederick can get used to getting
around. Your father was all right
before I left last night too.

KEITH HARDY
(Puzzled.)

What, before you left last night?
But who gave my father his

medication if the both of you left.
When Bunny and I returned home last
evening, I saw the kitchen light
on. Now, one of you had to here
to give my father his medication.
Wasn't it you, Frederick, who gave
the Judge his medicine?

PETE
(Steps forward.)

No, Pete, I was here, remember.
Frederick had already left before
your father died I presume, because
when I checked on him yesterday, he
was alive.

KEITH HARDY

INT: NERVOUSLY PACES THE GROUND BACK AND
FORTH.

No, no, no, it's all wrong, Pete!
You weren't the one who supposed to
have given my father his
medication.

(Points finger.)

I told you, Frederick, didn't I?

PETE
(Turns to everyone, interrupts.)

But, Mr. Keith, what difference
does it make who gave the Judge

his medication? Ah, I worked here
a long time, sir, and you've always
said that it didn't matter if I,
you, or Miss Bunny, or Monica, gave
the Judge his medication, just as
long as he received it, didn't you
Sir?

CORONER FINDING EVIDENCE IN JUDGE HARDY'S BEDROOM

Up in the Judge's bedroom, the county coroner of Running Creek, Alabama, didn't take long to establish the fact that Justice John Hardy almost certainly had committed suicide. The coroner also discovered at least five needle holes injections with ten times the prescribed dosage of medication, with 100 milligrams more than the normal amount that was prescribed to be administered for the Judge, the Coroner learned from a recent phone call he had made to the judge's pharmacist earlier. But, before returning outside to the waiting crowd to give his account of the time and cause of death, the coroner notices Justice John Hardy's pillow lying on the floor under the bed. He bent over and picked the pillow up off the floor with his latex gloves on, and turned the pillow over on its other side and discovered what looked like dried saliva and blood stains in the center of the pillow.

After putting the pillow in a plastic bag for further investigation, the coroner finally steps outside into the front yard of the house where there are mobs of neighbors, and the county news reporters start asking questions between each flash.

REPORTER 1

Can you tell us, Doctor, the cause
of Judge Hardy's death?

REPORTER 2

What about the motive Doctor, do
you think the Negroes killed the Judge?

REPORTER 3

If you don't think the Judge was
murdered, Doctor, does it look like
suicide?

REPORTER 4

There's another Negro working for
the Judge, Doctor, maybe he
murdered the Judge. Have you
taken that possibility into
account, Doctor?

SERIES OF SHOTS: REPORTERS- PETE AND FRED
HANDCUFFED-

ANGRY CROWD- CRIME SCENE.

DOCTOR

DOCTOR TAKES OFF HIS GLOVES.

PETE AND FREDERICK ARE HANDCUFFED TOGETHER
NEAR THE

DEPUTIES

Of course, sheriff, this is only my
assumption, but, I can't be sure of
anything until the autopsy....

SHERIFF

TOUCHES THE CORONER'S CHEST.

> Come on, Doctor, now, an autopsy!
> that's a waste of time, when we
> have the prime suspects right over
> there.

He points hack at Pete and Frederick without looking, who are now sitting in the back seat of the sheriff's car in the car!

> Now, you know, Doctor and I know,
> who probably murdered the Judge, if
> It was murder. Who else would have
> A motive to kill the Judge, but
> that " Negro boy" 'Frederick
> Harris," I tried to tell Keith
> that hiring that "Nigger," would
> be real dangerous after Judge
> Hardy sentence the boy and his wife
> to prison.

DOCTOR

EXT: SHERIFF- OUTSIDE COURTROOM- LARGE CROWD OF ANGRY NEIGHBORS CARRYING STICKS, BASEBALL BATS, CHAINS AND TRASH CANS, WHO ARE TRYING TO GET AT FREDERICK AND PETE SITTING IN THE CAR, AND HE LOOKS BACK AT THE SHERIFF.

> No, Sheriff, that' only a
> speculation right now, sir. A
> motive is only an assumption until
> it's proven.

SHERIFF

ANGRILY WALKS BACK AND FORTH, AND WALKS BACK
UP TO THE DOCTOR.

> Okay, okay, Doctor, okay, that may
> be true, but, turns around and
> looks over his shoulder to see if
> anyone's listening to him.
> This is off the record, but, I know
> it's only your professional
> assumption, but, do you think the
> Judge was murdered by one of the
> negroes?

THE END!

Writer:

Tyrone A. Fitzgerald
Michael L. Lewis Sr.
Andre Carr

Platinum Plus Inc.

EMAIL: RAHIM819@AOL.COM

Milton Keynes UK
Ingram Content Group UK Ltd.
UKHW050658280324
440307UK00012B/459